Bittersweet Brews

A Simple Love Story: Book 3

Dana LeCheminant

To those who brighten the world
by being a part of it

CHAPTER ONE

May 2018

Adam wasn't worried, so I made sure I was nervous enough for the both of us. That was the biggest problem working with a man like Adam Munroe. Most of the time he was cautious. Guarded. Most of the time nothing went wrong. But on those rare occasions he thought everything was great and we would have no trouble, things *always* went wrong.

"Matthew," Adam said, and I could feel him staring at me from the driver's seat of his Lexus where we waited. "Relax."

I never relaxed, and that was part of the reason he was still sitting there instead of six feet under. I had gotten him out of multiple scrapes over the years just by paying attention. As long as I thought we would encounter trouble, I could keep him alive. It was my job, after all. "We should have changed the meeting place," I said, keeping my eyes on the empty parking lot.

Sighing, Adam unclicked his seatbelt. "He had to catch a last minute flight. It only made sense to meet him on his way there."

I tapped my foot, a nervous habit I hadn't been able to conquer over the years. My brother Ben used to tell me I was only still when I was asleep, and sometimes even then I had a hard time not moving around. He constantly told me how annoying it was; I liked to think it was a sign of superior physiology and intellect. If I was holding still, it was usually because things were either very good or very, very bad. "So he's probably running from the feds and dumping all his stolen loot on us," I said under my breath. It wouldn't be the first time we'd crossed paths with criminals like that, and heaven knew it wouldn't be the last. "Where did he say he got the statue?" I asked louder.

"His grandmother brought it over from Sudan back in the thirties."

I laughed a little to myself. "Not Nigeria? That's a shocker."

"What is wrong with you today?"

Adam Munroe was my best friend, but sometimes he could be a pain in my—

"You're acting like we're about to be ambushed by petty thieves," Adam continued roughly, pulling my gaze to him. He didn't get angry often, so I'd quickly learned to pay attention when he was. "Do you really think I didn't do my homework? This is my job, Matt."

"And mine is to keep you safe," I replied. He had to have seen enough movies to know how idiotic the whole idea was. "You're sitting in an abandoned parking lot waiting to buy an ancient artifact that probably belongs in a museum."

"Exactly."

I narrowed my eyes as I stared at him. He wasn't the most expressive of men, but being around the guy nearly 24/7 meant I had learned to pick up on the little things. Like the flick of his eyes to his phone telling me he was hiding something and there was likely another party involved in the deal about to go down. That complicated things, and I was not prepared for this. "Adam," I growled. "What have you gotten yourself into?"

Rolling his eyes was a bit uncalled for. He was spending too much time with his wife. "Relax," he said again. "The Harvard Museum of Natural History knew Lanna was going to be in the area and—"

"Harvard?" A bit of a distance from California, I would say.

Adam scowled a little. "And they've been trying to track down this piece for months. I offered to retrieve it."

"*Retrieve* it? Adam, you're not some archaeologist superhero. You do art, and you're good at it. So you should stick to that." I tensed as a sleek black Escalade pulled into the lot on the other end and crawled toward us. "Assuming you make it out of this alive," I added as I slipped out of the car, Adam right behind me. It may have been a few years since anything actually dangerous had happened, but that didn't make me any less nervous.

The Escalade came to a stop about twenty yards from us, and three men stepped out. "On his way to the airport," I grumbled to myself.

"If they don't do it first, I'm going to kill you, Adam."

He had the nerve to smile. "I'm not sure threatening your sister's husband is a good idea," he said.

"I don't care. Which one is Sanford?"

"The one in the middle."

So that left the tall two on either side for me to keep an eye on. Not for the first time I wished I was a little taller. And bulkier. But the Davenport family certainly wasn't known for its size. Both of Sanford's meaty bodyguards stood mostly motionless, and their dark sunglasses hid which direction they kept their gazes. Still, the one on the right kept a little closer to Sanford, while the man on the left had his hands free. Righty was there to protect Sanford; Lefty would go after us.

"Thank you for meeting me," Sanford said as soon as the five of us met in the middle of our two cars. "I know it was inconvenient."

"That's one way to put it," I said under my breath. Lefty was a little too close for comfort.

Adam shook Sanford's hand, all calm and collected like he should be. At least during business transactions, he knew how to act the part of cool-headed man in charge. Normally Adam was more on the soft-spoken and shy side, which I had to admit was one of the reasons I loved the guy. He was perfect for my sister, even if he sometimes got himself into unnecessarily dangerous situations like this one. "I understand," Adam said. "We're all busy."

"Yes," Sanford agreed. His voice trembled, and I readied my hand to grab my gun if necessary. Lefty mirrored me. "If we could move this along…"

"You first," I said, gaining myself a soft groan from Adam.

Righty lifted a suitcase and pulled the lid open, revealing the little stone statue Adam was so eager to purchase, though I couldn't see why it was worth taking a risk like this. The Egyptian god-looking thing was barely a foot tall and looked about ready to fall apart, held together only by the molded foam it sat in. Sanford sniffed without looking at the suitcase, his eyes a little too watery given the cloudy morning sky and lack of wind. "There," he said, croaking a little. "Your turn."

Adam pulled his phone from his pocket and started typing, and I cleared my throat. Glancing at me, he took a breath then continued, typing a few extra strokes. *Good.* He added in the failsafe I'd set up for him, just in case. He had hated the idea at first, but at least he was willing to use it when it mattered most. "It should all be there," he said, lifting his eyes to Sanford.

Lefty shifted, sliding his right foot back half an inch. Righty was closing the suitcase but much too tense, and Sanford nearly dropped his phone as he grabbed it to make sure Adam's money was in his account. "That looks..." He swallowed. *It can't be that hard to say, Sanford.* "Fan-fantastic." Then he gave the subtlest of nods to his men.

I grabbed my gun at the same time Lefty gripped his, both of us pointing our weapons at the other's boss. "Stand down!" I shouted as I stepped in front of Adam.

Sanford was already backing away, fumbling to grab the suitcase from Righty, and if I let him get to the car, we were screwed. But if I moved to get a better shot, Lefty would drop Adam within the second. Just the way he held his gun told me he was military trained, and I wasn't about to underestimate his aim.

"Sanford!" I snarled. He was almost to the Escalade with that stupid suitcase. We were going to lose the statue! That piece of junk was the whole reason we were here, and Adam clearly thought it was important. Odds were slim anyone would be able to track it down again if I let it go. I had one chance. I stepped and pulled the trigger, knocking the suitcase from Sanford's hand. But mine wasn't the only shot. Lefty had already turned to run back to the car, and Adam's cry of pain froze me to the core. "No!" I cried.

Adam fell backwards before I could catch him, landing hard on the pavement as the Escalade squealed from the parking lot. Blood soaked his chest. He was still breathing, but barely.

"Adam!" I shouted, dropping at his side. "Adam, talk to me."

He couldn't keep his eyes open. There was too much blood. I'd seen wounds like this before in the Army, and...

"Hospital," I whispered as my hands shook almost too badly for me to grab my phone. It rang way too many times before the emergency operator picked up. "I need an ambulance," I said breathlessly. "GSW. 1507 West Yarndale. Hurry! Adam." I grabbed his hand, holding tight. "Adam, stay with me. Please. Just hang on. You can't die on me, man. Oh God, please don't die on me."

Adam nodded once, and then he stopped breathing.

I'd never liked hospitals. When I was seventeen, I spent an agonizing six hours sitting in a cold waiting room wondering if my older brother was going to live, the whole time knowing he wasn't because he'd been crushed by a pickup truck while trying to save his boss from the collision. My parents—some of the highest among the social elites of San Francisco—had been at an event and didn't answer their phones, and my sister was too young, so I'd taken on the task of waiting. No seventeen-year-old should have to peek through a little window and watch a team of sterile surgeons try to fix something unfixable. No kid should have to be the one to tell his family his brother was dead.

My sister Lanna thought Ben died on the scene. She was only fourteen at the time, and she didn't need to know he'd spent his last hours of life in complete agony. She took the news harder than my parents, who were too high and mighty to show grief, and for a while I worried she was never going to get over losing her protector. I knew then just as I knew now that she needed Benjamin a lot more than she needed me, and I would have given anything to trade places with my big brother.

Just like I desperately wished I could do now.

Lanna was, understandably, a mess. A blue-scrubbed doctor had come out an hour ago and told us Adam was out of surgery and things were looking good, but I'd never seen her pace like this. She'd crossed the length of the waiting room about a thousand times and wouldn't even look at me, not that I blamed her. Her husband was clinging to life because I couldn't do my job. I would hate me too.

"Why won't they let us see him?" she asked after her latest rotation around the room.

I kept my gaze on the floor. I couldn't bear to see the pain in her eyes or the tightness of her lips as she fought back tears. "He's in recovery, Lanna," I said, my voice hoarse. "Give him time." Time he wouldn't need if I hadn't failed. I should have taken Lefty out first, *then* tried to secure the artifact. Only an idiot would leave a gun in play.

"I just want to *see* him," she continued. "Can't they at least tell me…" She stopped, and I looked up as a young nurse came our way.

The girl smiled, putting her hand on Lanna's shoulder. "Your husband is awake, Mrs. Munroe. He's asking for you."

Lanna exhaled with relief, a good deal of tension slipping from her shoulders as she rushed off to follow the nurse. Only because she paused in the hallway and waved me after her did I follow. I doubted either my sister or Adam would want me there in that room, but they were both too kind to say so. I'd just make an appearance, express my sincerest apology, and get out of their way like I should have done years ago.

Adam looked terrible, grey and sickly and attached to a plastic tube keeping him alive. But at least he *was* alive. No thanks to me. Lanna pulled a chair as close to the bed as she could and gripped his hand as if her own life depended on it, and he gazed at her in a way that made me sick inside. I'd almost separated them from each other. Forever. Adam and Lanna Munroe were a fairytale couple, and I'd almost destroyed them.

"Where's Benny?" Adam whispered.

Lanna brushed away a tear from her cheek. "He's with my mom. She said she can keep him as long as we need so I can stay here with you."

My nephew had hardly spent an hour away from Lanna or Adam since he was born, and I could only imagine the uproar the toddler was making for my poor mom who hadn't even taken care of her own kids. Before Lanna married Adam, not even in my wildest dreams could I see dear Mom changing a diaper or dealing with a tantrum. She left that to whichever nanny we had at the time. Things had certainly changed in recent years, but that didn't make her any more equipped to handle Benny for more than a few hours. I'd have to relieve her soon.

"Matt."

I blinked, realizing Adam was looking at me. *Not yet.* I hadn't figured out my apology.

"Thanks."

I blinked again, not entirely sure I heard his whisper right. "What?"

His lips twitched in what I thought was an attempted smile. *But why?* "You saved my life."

Ha. Of course I didn't. I was the reason he was hurt in the first place, but I knew better than to argue something like this. So I gave him a smile back and left the room.

I had to get out of the hospital.

I drove across the city without fully paying attention to where I went. All I could think about was Adam's blood on my hands as I kept him alive with CPR while I waited for the ambulance and how close I'd come to making my baby sister a widow and how I *knew* better than to care more about a little statue than my own family. I had put in that failsafe so Adam would have to add a second authorization before the funds fully transferred, which made it easier for me to do my job. At least it should have. His money was safe, but he was not. And it was my fault.

I pulled into the cemetery, not surprised by my subconscious destination. I couldn't even count the number of times I'd been there, often enough over the years that I should have had my own parking spot by now. Most of my darkest days had happened at this cemetery, but that had never stopped me from coming back again and again.

I really shouldn't have come. I had my mother to rescue and a three-year-old to entertain and an investigation into Sanford to deal with. But right now, I needed to chat with my brother.

Ben's grave wasn't with the other Davenports, but I'd chosen this location for a reason. Even at seventeen, I knew I would be spending a lot of time here, so while my parents pretended life was normal, leaving all the funeral planning to me, I picked a gravesite with a sturdy tree at its feet so I could sit against the trunk and talk for hours, something I'd done many times since. By the time my parents realized what I had done, it was too late, and it was probably one of the main factors in them disinheriting me. I didn't deserve to be a Davenport, they'd told me, and I was fine with that. I didn't want to be like them anyway.

I still wasn't sure I deserved to be a Davenport. It wasn't like I had lived up to the name.

I sat in my usual spot, glad that the early afternoon sun had dried the dew, and I took a deep breath as my eyes locked on the granite headstone in front of me.

"Hey, Ben," I said. I sounded as awful as I had at the hospital, my voice hoarse and weak. It had been a long day and would only get longer as soon as I got back to reality. "Something bad happened today. I nearly got Adam killed, and…" I swallowed. "You should have seen Lanna's face when she got to the hospital. I've never seen her so scared in my life. It was worse than…" Worse than when Luke died. It had been almost six years since my best friend died protecting my sister, and I still couldn't bring myself to say his name out loud. Lanna had been in love with him, but she had had Adam to help her through her grief. I had no one but Ben.

Plucking a blade of grass, I sighed and shook my head as I tore the grass into little pieces. "I know you'd tell me it wasn't my fault," I continued, "but you weren't there. I *knew*, Ben. I knew if I turned my focus to Sanford, the other guy would go after Adam. I made the wrong choice, and it almost got him killed."

Ben wouldn't have been so stupid. My older brother was always quiet, but he was the smartest man I knew and would have done everything he could to keep Adam safe. His selflessness was admirable to a fault. It was, after all, what got him killed. He would have known how to comfort Lanna too, but I just sat there and let her pace because no joke could make those hours of waiting easier. My limited skill set was useless at the hospital, and my sister suffered because of it.

"Don't look at me like that," I told the headstone. "I'm not going to fall off the wagon. Adam's alive, at least." Besides, if I turned to drinking like I had after Ben died, that wouldn't help anyone. Those ten years had been the darkest of my life and still haunted me. My little sister had nearly been so emotionally manipulated by my mother that she couldn't even function like a normal adult, and that wouldn't have happened if I had just been the brother she needed me to be instead of drowning my sorrows in a bottle and shutting out the world. No amount of misery, no matter how heavy it weighed on me, would lead me down that avenue again.

"I really messed up, Ben," I said, dropping my head against the tree behind me. "What if…what if the ambulance hadn't gotten there in time? I would have lost my best friend and probably my sister all at once. And Mom would have killed me, considering how perfect she thinks Adam Munroe is."

My phone buzzed in my pocket, and I knew who was calling before I even saw the name. "Speak of the devil. Hey, Mom."

"Matthew!" she said loudly, though I could hardly hear her over the high-pitched screaming in the background. "How's Adam?" Little Benny was certainly making her life fun at the moment.

"Alive," I replied.

"Well that's a relief. Ben, please, can you not—Matthew, I need—Benny, don't touch that! Gramma is trying to—Matthew, please."

I sighed, pushing myself to my feet. "I'm on my way," I told her. Brother chat was over for the day. Pocketing my phone, I said my goodbyes to Ben's grave then followed the familiar path back to my car, my eyes on my feet and my hands in my pockets. It was barely three o'clock, but I was already exhausted. Adding a tantruming toddler to the mix was going to be the perfect storm for a migraine, but it was the least I could do for Lanna, considering I was the reason she was at the hospital in the first place. I just had to push through the tiredness and—

Something solid and oddly fragrant suddenly smashed into me, complete with tiny sharp pains in my arms and a shouted curse I'd never heard in a cemetery before. Stumbling back a step, I found myself face to face with a young woman who held the remains of what had been a bouquet of roses and was now a few broken twigs and half a dozen thorns pricks in my skin.

"Watch where you're going, idiot," she said loudly, her green-eyed glare as icy as her words. The freckles on her nose and the green converse shoes she wore made her look pretty young, but I had no doubt she had a mean bite to go with that bark of hers.

"Sorry," I mumbled, plucking a few tiny spikes from my arm. The day just kept getting better. "I have a lot on my mind."

I tried to scoot past her, but she stepped in my way and brandished her twigs. "These are useless now," she said. She had a couple of leaves in her dark hair, but I decided not to point them out. I was pretty sure that wouldn't exactly help the situation.

"Sorry," I said again. What more did she expect me to say? "I have to get somewhere. I'm sorry." First my sister and her husband, and now I was disappointing complete strangers. Now all I needed was for my nephew to forget I was his favorite uncle—never mind I was his *only* uncle—and scream at me too.

Leaving the still fuming woman behind with her mess of thorns and petals, I hurried the rest of the way from the cemetery and slipped into my car, allowing myself one deep breath before setting out for the rest of a very long day. After my mistake this morning, I had a lot of damage to undo.

CHAPTER TWO

"Benjamin Lucas Munroe, you get back here!" Lanna's whispered shout was answered by a shrill giggle that jolted more than one person awake, myself included. She was already unbuckling her seatbelt to go after the escapee, but I touched her arm and with a look told her to stay in her seat.

"I'll get him," I said and slipped into the aisle.

The toddler was halfway to economy class already, and though there wasn't too much trouble he could get into on an airplane, I couldn't imagine the flight attendants enjoying a three-foot terror on the loose. Or the other passengers. I snatched him up just before he reached the partition and lifted him up to eye level with mock anger.

"Now where do you think you're going, you rascal?" I asked quietly. Though it wasn't a late flight, most people had fallen asleep during the six-hour journey, and I didn't want to add their annoyance to Lanna's stress level. She was struggling as it was. Benny wasn't often a troublesome kid—pretty angelic usually—but with his dad still stuck in the hospital the last few days, he had been acting out more and more.

Grinning, Benny struggled in my arms but luckily didn't fight much. "I want to see the plane!" he said.

"I know, bud. But you have to stay in your seat."

He shook his head violently, not that I could blame him. Even in first class, airplanes were confining, and Benny had an energy level that far exceeded his parents' and made me wonder where it came from. He wanted to run around and play with toys and have an endless lawn to roll around on. Instead he was flying clear across the country to see someone he didn't often interact with. The original plan had been to leave him at home with Adam, but that was no longer an option.

I could see Lanna peering back from her seat, so I put on a smile and pulled Benny close. "I have an idea," I said, putting as much energy into my words as I could. "Why don't we look out the window, and you can show me all the dogs you see."

His eyes went wide. "There are dogs?" he asked.

"You have to hunt for them," I told him, making my way back to my seat. "They're playing hide and seek down there, and you have to find them!"

He went to the window immediately and pressed his face against the glass. *Thank goodness.* I had maybe five minutes max before my game stopped working, considering we were 30,000 feet in the air. But he was a smart kid who happened to absolutely adore dogs, and he wouldn't waste an opportunity to see one.

"Thanks," Lanna said in front of me. "I've just been so tired lately, and I fell asleep for just a second."

I was pretty sure she'd barely slept at all over the last couple of days. More than tired, she looked exhausted, worse than I'd ever seen her. Not having Adam at her side was taking its toll.

"I'll find him, Lanna," I said. Sanford was not going to get away with what he did to Adam. There was just one problem. When not babysitting, I'd spent every waking moment helping the police track down Sanford and his goons, and we'd gotten nowhere. But she didn't need to know that. "I'm not going to rest until we catch him."

She frowned as she curled up in her seat with her blanket up to her chin. "Matthew," she said, "I don't want this to turn into another Catherine situation."

Her words may have been mumbled because she was half asleep, but they still hit me hard. Our cousin Catherine had been kidnapped on our watch, and Lanna had spent the three days before we found her worried to the point where she couldn't eat or sleep. Having to see her at that level of suffering while I struggled to find Catherine had nearly destroyed me, and I wasn't sure either of us could go through that again. At least we knew where Adam was, but finding Sanford was likely the only way she'd be able to sleep easy again.

"Why does this keep happening?" she asked.

A lump settled in my throat, but I tried to make sure I sounded like I meant my words when I said, "I'm sorry, Lanna." Eventually I would figure out how to make her feel safe. "I'm doing everything I can."

She yawned, closing her eyes. "Don't do that to yourself, Matthew," she mumbled. "Seth is taking care of it."

And suddenly I couldn't breathe. "What?" I asked, trying to sound like she hadn't just stabbed a knife into my gut. "I thought Seth was in Uzbekistan."

"He is," she replied. "He's better at this kind of thing, though."

Before I could choke out a reply, Benny said my name, the word muffled because he spoke into the window. "I don't see any dogs," he complained.

I sat there frozen, Lanna's words still slamming into me hard because she thought I wasn't capable of finding Sanford, and she had given the task to a super soldier on the other side of the world. She was already asleep again, but her comment rang in my ears until my head hurt.

And Benny pounded his hand against my shoulder and said, "No dogs, Matt!"

Letting out my breath, I patted his arm and sighed. Time was running out for this game, so I would have to find another way to entertain him so Lanna could sleep. She needed it. "Keep looking. I think I see one right down there." Once we landed in Boston, there would be plenty of things to keep his attention, and hopefully he would sleep during the drive to the hotel. Then maybe we could figure out how we were going to handle the events of the next day.

As long as my family survived the weekend in one piece, I would consider it a win. After the incident with Sanford and his goons, my standard for success had gone way down.

"Auntie Catherine is graduating college!" Lanna told Benny, though I doubted he had any idea what that meant. "We get to clap for her when she comes on the stage. Can you practice clapping for me?" She held the boy in her arms as we waited just outside the mass of chairs set up in the courtyard. We would sit right before the ceremony began, just in case Benny got restless quickly. At least Lanna slept last night and looked better than yesterday, though I suspected some of that was because of the phone call from Adam a few minutes earlier. She said he sounded stronger and was up and walking around the hospital a bit, which brought a little life back into her eyes.

At least someone had managed to make her feel a little better.

While Lanna played with her son, I scanned the crowd. I wasn't expecting any trouble, not this far from home, but I'd learned my lesson. Plan for the worst, and nothing could go wrong. Aside from the occasional person trying to track down their family members, most of the crowd were smiles and happiness. This was, after all, a happy occasion.

Although, the balding man in the ridiculously expensive Italian suit not far from us looked decidedly uncomfortable, and I scowled in his direction.

Lanna saw him too. "What is *he* doing here?" she asked.

"Begging to get punched," I growled. "I'll be right back."

"Don't get blood on your shirt," she said, and I bit back the pain of that comment. She didn't think I could even take care of one self-absorbed elite with an entitlement complex. No wonder she asked Seth to track down Sanford.

I stopped just next to the man, pretending to look out over the crowd for a moment so I could convince myself I could actually handle this simple confrontation. "What are you doing here, Uncle Milton?" I finally asked.

He jumped and turned toward me, though I kept my gaze straight ahead. "Matthew," he acknowledged coldly. "My daughter is graduating. I have every right to be here."

"Funny," I replied. "I don't think Catherine sent you an invitation." In fact, my cousin had forbidden any of us from mentioning the event to her father. The man had visited his only child just once or twice in the last four years and was probably only here to make a public appearance and pretend to be a proud father. Clearly he thought looking the part was enough to convince people he was not the sort of man who still hadn't spoken to his daughter about when she was kidnapped by a literal terrorist four years ago. He'd been too busy enjoying his honeymoon with his now third ex-wife to take the time to answer his phone. After we realized how terrible a father he was, we had decided to let him learn about it on his own instead of filling him in on the details. My own parents hadn't been great, but they would have at least checked their messages after leaving their children for a month.

Milton sniffed, straightening his suit. "I have every right," he repeated.

"I'm going to have to ask you to leave," I said.

Chuckling, he looked me over once and rolled his eyes, sending a wave of anger through me. "What's a good-for-nothing drunk like you going to do, kid? Wave your arms a bit and scare me off campus with your breath? I doubt you could even move me if you tried."

I clenched my fists. I hadn't been a drunk in years. *Oh, I'll tell you what I'll do. I'll—*

"Nah, that's my job," a deep voice said behind us, and my anger shifted to frustration and annoyance. What the hell was *he* doing here? He was supposed to be in Central Asia. Uncle Milton and I both turned to greet the man who literally cast a shadow over us.

Seth Hastings, for all his admirable qualities, was intimidating, and he knew it. Six foot eight and built like an incredibly fit ox, he stood there with arms folded and jaw tight as his eyes lasered right into Milton's. "What are you doing here, Davenport?" he asked, speaking my same question but getting a very different response.

Milton practically quivered where he stood looking up into the battle-worn face of one of the country's best soldiers. "I, uh, I just thought…"

Seth shifted his not insignificant weight to one foot, dropping his fists to his side. He was going for a casual look, but anyone who saw his face would know there was nothing casual about this man. "You thought you would ruin Cat's day by turning her celebration into a photo op," he finished for him.

"That's what I was going to say," I mumbled under my breath.

Milton shrugged, but the motion was tense and stiff. "I have every right to—"

"You lost that right thirteen years ago when you left your own child parentless," Seth countered. "Now I suggest you leave before I make you leave. You'll still get that photo op you want, only I don't think it will work in your favor." He nodded to several people in the nearby crowd who had pulled out their phones in the hopes of capturing some exciting footage.

Milton paled and practically scurried off as if Seth had given him a very short countdown. I hated knowing I would never be able to inspire that sort of fear in *anyone*. Given the fact that my whole job was about intimidating people before they could do Adam harm of any kind, I was starting to question my career choice. My conversation with Lanna on the plane hadn't helped.

"There's the coward we know and love," Seth muttered, his keen eyes following my uncle until he disappeared from view.

I tried to save my dignity. "I was just about to—"

"I know." Grinning, Seth clapped me on the back and nearly knocked me off my feet.

Coughing, I straightened up and asked, "What are you doing here, Seth? I thought you were on a mission." Seth had been in the Special Forces for years and seemed to always be off saving the world somehow. It was ridiculously dangerous, and I had always been jealous. There was no way in hell I would ever be able to pull off being the Green Beret equivalent of James Bond. Not like he did.

He led the way back toward Lanna, completely unaware—or not caring—that his mere size parted the crowd for us as they quickly moved out of the way of the giant casually strolling through their midst.

"I *was* on a mission," he said. "Am. They'll be fine without me."

My eyes went wide. Given some of his more recent missions, I was pretty sure abandoning his team wasn't exactly a smart move. It was bad enough that Lanna had him looking for Sanford as well. "Seth, don't you think you should have stayed—"

"Are you kidding?" His hard exterior suddenly melted into nothing but excitement and happiness, the real Seth behind the soldier mask, and quite a few people stared at him as the change left them totally befuddled. I knew their pain; it had taken me over a year to realize that beneath his hardened shell, Seth had a kind heart and a gentle soul. Honestly, I still hadn't figured out how he managed to do his job without losing the light inside of him.

"My girlfriend is graduating MIT at the top of her class after only three years," he said lightly. "There is no way I would miss this. Lanna!"

Lanna's face immediately brightened as she caught sight of the tank, and she jumped into his smothering hug and disappeared behind his massive arms. "Seth! I didn't think you would make it. Does Catherine know?"

He laughed, the sound carrying and drawing even more attention our way than before. "It's like you don't know me at all," he teased.

Lanna grinned. "How are you going to surprise her?"

"I'll let you know once I figure out how best to embarrass her," he replied, matching her smile.

I hadn't been able to get a real smile out of my sister in days, and

Seth had been here for all of thirty seconds. Even Benny looked excited to see the soldier, though I was pretty sure he had only met Seth a few times. I could never actually bring myself to hate Seth Hastings, given the fact that he saved my cousin's life after she was kidnapped, but times like these brought me close. Could the man be any more perfect?

"Oh, Lanna," Seth said as we took our seats before the graduation ceremony started, "I was asking around about this Sanford guy, and I think we've got a lead on where he might be hiding. I have some contacts looking into it and should hear back in a couple of hours."

Tears pooled in her eyes as she held Benny close and whispered, "Seth, that's amazing. Thank you."

I clenched my fists, hiding them at my side. After all the time I had spent trying to give my sister even a glimmer of hope, she thought I was useless. Without even trying, Seth had given my sister something to smile about.

I sat through the painfully long ceremony in silence, clapping when appropriate and doing everything I could to not scowl as Seth managed to both entertain Benny and keep Lanna smiling as we waited for Catherine's name to be called. No one could quite make a man feel useless like Seth could, and though I knew Catherine would be beyond excited when she saw him, I was starting to really hate the fact that he was here. If I had known he would be in Boston, maybe I would have stayed back in California with Benny and let Lanna enjoy the ceremony without having to worry about anyone but herself.

Except, I would have hated to miss this. Catherine was like a second sister, and she'd spent every summer and Christmas with us since high school. At least when Seth was off on his top-secret missions, she came to me for companionship, so I liked to think I wasn't entirely unwelcome. I had, regrettably, been a little overbearing when we first met, though that was mainly because she'd been attempting to escape to the other side of the world at the time. We'd grown closer over the last few years, and I was proud of her. I wanted to share this moment with her, no matter how inadequate Seth made me feel.

"Catherine Davenport," the dean said, and nearly half the crowd of graduates—and a good portion of the guests, I noticed—jumped to their feet with cheers and applause, though I shouldn't have been surprised. Catherine was nothing if not social. Seth's whistle overpowered every cheer, and halfway through shaking the dean's hand, Catherine froze and looked out over the crowd as if she recognized Seth just from a whistle, though we were definitely too far away for her to see us in the bright sun.

"Ha!" Seth said as we sat again. "That's going to drive her crazy." And he looked absolutely pleased with that result.

I couldn't help but smile with him. Seth's good-natured personality was infectious. "You're torturing her?" I asked, and I could picture Catherine retaking her seat and trying to look behind her into the mass of guests.

"It's good for her," he replied and pulled out his phone. He found a picture of him and another soldier posing with some kids and a soccer ball, and he quickly posted it online with the caption, "Going to bed sore tonight after getting absolutely demolished by these future pros." Snorting with amusement, he leaned a little closer to me so we could watch for the comment we both knew would come quickly.

Miss you! Catherine posted after only a few seconds.

I clicked my tongue in mock disappointment. "On her phone at her own graduation," I said. "What are we going to do with her?"

"Will you boys be nice?" Lanna scolded, though she was smiling too. Catherine had grown up a lot over the years, but she hadn't yet kicked the habit of always keeping her phone on her and staying connected to her loved ones. If I had gone through what she had, I would probably be the same way. Those few days after she was abducted, when she was trapped with no communication with the outside world, it had nearly killed me not knowing if she was even alive. I could only imagine how that felt on her end. If not for Seth looking after her after she escaped her captor, Catherine wouldn't have come back to us.

I *really* wanted to hate him sometimes. But I never could and never would. Not when he was the best thing to ever happen to my pseudo-sister.

The ceremony ended just as Benny started to get restless, and we joined the rest of the guests in waiting for the graduates to come find their families. Lanna took her son off to the side a little so he could play in the grass, and Seth—who was almost a foot taller than me and could actually see over the crowd—kept an eye out for Catherine. I stood around useless.

"There she is," Seth said and immediately ducked down so he was hidden behind a small family. "Be right back," he continued then vanished into the crowd in half a second. How did he even *do* that? The man was huge, but he'd become completely invisible. No wonder the Army refused to let him go. A pity. I was sure Catherine would appreciate him not being on the other side of the world all the time.

"Catherine!" I called when she started scanning the sea of people. "Over here!"

It took her nearly five minutes just to cross the last little bit of distance to get to us because people kept offering her congratulations, but Catherine—as always—didn't mind the attention. Before Seth helped her set her priorities straight, attention had once been her ultimate goal in life.

"Matthew," she greeted and threw her arms around my shoulders with enough enthusiasm to knock me back a step or two. I doubted Seth ever had that problem. "I'm so glad you came! How's Adam doing?"

I couldn't find the words, so I nodded to Lanna.

My sister pulled Catherine into a hug before she responded. "Better," she said after she'd gotten her fill of the embrace. "He's walking around now."

"I'm so glad to hear that." Catherine's eyes quickly scanned the immediate area, looking for Seth even though she thought he was off in some third world country saving lives one soccer game at a time. "Just make sure he doesn't carry anyone up a mountain," she continued, a little wilted, "and he'll be fine."

Seth slipped through a throng of people just behind her, his smile wide and altogether out of place for a man looking like he belonged in a mainstream action movie. "You're never going to let me live that down, are you?" he asked.

Catherine shrieked and spun right into Seth's hold, and he smoothly bent down and kissed her, much to the dismay of many of the men and women nearby, I noticed with a chuckle. I'd thought Lanna and Adam were bad, but Seth and Catherine added celebrity crushes to their list of enviable qualities and could get entire rooms to fall in love with both of them with nothing but a couple of smiles.

Clearing my throat, I pulled their attention away from each other. "People are watching," I reminded them.

"That's never stopped me before," Catherine joked, but her cheeks turned quite red as she fell against Seth's chest and into his protective hold. It was her favorite place to be, I'd quickly realized, so I'd stopped trying to keep them apart at the beginning of their relationship.

It didn't take long for me to decide Seth wasn't anything like the tabloids had painted him, and Catherine in wisdom beyond her years decided they should only be friends, at least until she finished high school. He was as safe as they came, and Catherine was happy. That was all that mattered.

"So how does it feel to be a college graduate?" Lanna asked, lifting a suddenly sleepy Benny into her arms.

I immediately took the toddler from her, knowing how heavy he could get when asleep, and she gave me a grateful smile that boosted my confidence just a little. So I wasn't *totally* useless.

"Ready to conquer the world?" Seth added.

Catherine rolled her eyes. "A bachelor's degree in linguistics is worthless without a Ph.D.," she said. "I have a long way to go before I can even think of applying for the FBI."

Seth turned so he was holding her from behind, looking altogether too happy about how easily she latched onto his arms around her shoulders. He may have been gone a lot, but they never seemed to miss a beat with each other. "I'm pretty sure they'll start hounding you long before then," he assured her and touched a kiss to the top of her head. "Everyone. FBI. CIA. The Navy. They would all be lucky to have you. But I draw the line at Interpol. They're the worst."

"You know," Catherine said thoughtfully, "I *did* just get a very interesting phone call from someone at Interpol. She had a lot to say about their—"

"Don't even think about it," Seth warned, though he saw through her joke and smiled even wider. Then, without warning, his expression slid into complete sincerity, and he stepped around so he could look Catherine in the eye. "I can only imagine the sleep I'd lose knowing you were traveling who knows where. I don't... I don't think I could handle it."

Catherine reached up and ran her thumb along a scar that cut across his cheekbone to his ear. "Now you know how I feel every day you're not here," she whispered. "I can't look out for you if you're on the other side of the world."

"Cat..."

Lanna touched my arm, indicating with a jerk of her head that we should give them a little privacy. But I stayed put, a thought forming quickly in my mind. Maybe I couldn't protect my family like I'd once thought, but I knew who could.

"Hey, Seth," I said, "can I talk to you for a second?"

Neither he nor Catherine really wanted me interrupting their serious conversation, but Seth nodded and joined me just out of earshot of the ladies. "Something wrong?" he asked, reading my face.

"Not exactly," I replied, shifting Benny to my other arm. "I have something to ask you."

Seth narrowed his eyes a little. "I feel like I should be worried," he said, though I was pretty sure he was more confused than anything.

This wasn't going to be easy, so I had to just go ahead and say it before I changed my mind. "I want you to have my job."

Frowning, he glanced at Catherine then looked back at me. "Your job?" he repeated. "Working for Adam?"

I nodded. "Look, obviously I'm not cut out for it anymore, but—" He tried to protest, but I kept going. "But he's not going to stop doing his job just because a bullet got in his way once. He needs someone looking after him, and I can't…" I took a deep breath. "There's no one better than you, Seth." And I meant that literally. I doubted there was anyone in the world who was quite as strong or smart or caring as the man who'd fallen in love with my cousin, and there was no one I could trust quite as easily. "Seth, please. I need your help. At least until I can find someone worth his salt to take over."

He still frowned, but his expression carried a hint of thoughtfulness as he glanced at Catherine again. "She's considering Stanford so she can be closer to home," he muttered. "And I'm starting to think I'm a little too old for the Special Forces."

Oh please, if he thought *he* was getting old, that made me positively ancient. The man was only thirty.

"But I don't want to overstep my bounds," he continued, giving me a pointed look. Apparently he thought I was stepping aside for him.

Really, I was stepping aside *because* of him. After that conversation on the plane and now that I was standing in Seth's shadow—literally— I realized just how ineffective I was at protecting the people I loved. I was better suited for holding sleeping three-year-olds and running errands and making sure my dad actually ate dinner when he worked late nights. I had been reduced to a nanny, which sounded about right. Ben had been the one destined for greatness, not me.

"Honestly, Seth," I said, "I'm hoping to branch out a little bit. Take a break. Find something a little less stressful for a while."

"Yeah, you do look a little worn down," he muttered.

I glared at him.

"Are you sure, Matt? I know you love your job."

I *did* love my job. Up until I nearly got my brother-in-law killed. "I'm sure," I said. "You think you can get out of the Army, or will they make you go back?"

He snorted, and the sound made Catherine and Lanna both relax. I hadn't even realized they were tense about my whispered conversation, and I felt terrible for making them worry. I was making a mess of everything, apparently. "Don't fret, little man," Seth said and shoved his hands into his pockets as he took leisurely steps back to Catherine and grinned back at me. "The Army only like to pretend they tell me what to do, but I'm really the one in charge."

It was meant to be a joke, but I didn't doubt him. When it came to Seth Hastings, he was at the top of every food chain.

CHAPTER THREE

"Matt, don't be an idiot." When I first met him, Adam Munroe would have fainted at the thought of insulting someone, least of all someone who worked for him. Oh, how things had changed.

I just had to hold my ground long enough to convince him my plan was the best option, and then everything would work out. It had to. "Adam," I said calmly, "I've given this a lot of thought."

"Obviously not enough." If he wasn't confined to his bed for the next hour, I could imagine Adam grabbing me by the shoulder and trying to shake some sense into me. I had to hand it to him; getting shot had really given him a sense of backbone with me he hadn't had before. "Matthew Davenport, I'm not going to get rid of you just because some lowlife tried to double-cross me. If anything, the whole thing was my fault."

"Whoa." I held up a hand, making sure he caught the whole of my glare. "There is no way in hell I'm letting you blame yourself for any of this."

Adam tried to match my anger, but he still hadn't quite mastered that one. He was too good underneath it all to really put any power behind the expression. "I hope you don't talk like that around my son," he warned.

I rolled my eyes. "Adam," I said, "I'm not going to back down on this. You need someone to protect you, and that can't be me. Not anymore. Seth is perfectly capable of—"

"I know what Seth is," Adam growled, "and that's the problem. Nevermind he's so intimidating that no clients will want to talk to me, but can you imagine what people will think when they see I've switched to a bigger and better…" He froze, his eyes going wide. Apparently his filter had been damaged when he got shot, and he had lost his ability to keep his deeper thoughts to himself, since I could tell he hadn't meant to say that.

But he'd thought it all the same.

I gritted my teeth against the accidental insult, but it wasn't like he was wrong. Seth Hastings was everything I wasn't. "I thought you didn't care what people think," I said quietly, lowering my gaze to my feet. I knew Adam well enough to know that he would now try everything to bolster my confidence and convince me I was just as impressive as Catherine's Hulk, so I had to keep the conversation away from me as long as I could.

Adam's reply was just as soft as my comment. "I don't care. But people talk. And rumor will travel that I'm taking on dangerous jobs, so no one will want to buy. This could ruin Munroe Royalties, Matt."

"You'll be fine," I grumbled. No one worked the art industry as well as Adam.

"But will you?"

I looked up, the scrutiny of Adam's stare making my chest tighten. "I'll be fine," I said.

"What will you do?"

Though I took his question as a sign that he was starting to agree to my plan to have Seth take over for me, I really didn't like the turn the conversation had taken. Mostly because I didn't have an answer. It wasn't that I needed the money, since my trust fund from my wealthy family had me covered for the rest of my life, but I certainly couldn't spend all day doing nothing.

Sighing, Adam settled back against his pillows and slowly rubbed the ache out of his shoulder. I'd gotten him too worked up, and Lanna would likely get after me for making his injury worse. "Can't you just…" He looked out the window. "Can't you at least stay until you find something else?"

"You're going to be out of commission for at least another week, Adam. There's no better time than now to start looking."

He accepted that argument, nodding at the window as he continued to think the plan over. "And Seth's okay with it?" he asked, turning his gaze back to me.

I had to smile at that one. "I don't think I've ever seen him happier," I said. "This gives him the perfect way to stay close to Catherine without feeling like he's giving up on the world. And I think he really does want a quieter life." Of course, quiet for Seth was clearly too much for me.

"Matt, I..." He shook his head. "I don't want you to go. You're my best friend."

"I know." And under my breath I added, "Maybe I shouldn't be." My best friends—first my brother Ben, and then Luke Hawthorne six years ago—had a habit of dying on me. Adam had come way too close for comfort, and I was starting to think maybe the world would be better off if I didn't have friends.

"I just hope you know you can always come back," Adam continued. "There's nothing that says I can't have two bodyguards."

My smile felt forced this time, but I hoped Adam was too tired to notice. "We'll see," I said, though I had no intention of letting him put any part of his life in my hands. "It's not like I'm really going anywhere. You still have the unfortunate pleasure of having me for a brother-in-law."

Though Adam laughed a little, his eyes drooped. Time for me to leave.

"Get some sleep, Adam. I'll see you around."

I walked the hospital hallways slowly, my thoughts too jumbled to really have any direction. Adam's question—*What will you do?*—was the one I'd been asking myself ever since we got back from Boston. Right out of high school, I signed up for the Army. As soon as I could get out, I went straight to working for Adam, minus a bit of a rough patch in the middle I constantly tried to forget. It wasn't like I had a lot of skills on my resume, and I'd never taken the time to figure out what I wanted to do with the rest of my life. Oddly enough, when you have parents who dictate your every move, you don't gain a whole lot of independence until you're actually out in the world.

Dad would suggest I shadow him at work, start looking into becoming a lawyer like him. But for how shy and quiet he was, his job required he be ruthless, and I'd never seen myself anything like that side of him. Mom would tell me I needed to focus more on the social scene like she'd done most of her life. "You need a wife," she'd told me more than once, and apparently the best place to find one was at charity events and garden parties. Too bad all the women there were glammed up nightmares wrapped in plastic surgery. No, I had no intention of finding a wife among the elite and the wealthy.

I didn't really have *any* intention to find a wife. If I couldn't even protect Adam when I was fully alert and focused, how was I supposed to take care of a family?

Leaving my car at the hospital, I took to walking the streets. The late afternoon sun was warm but not unbearable, and the sounds of the city would help distract me so I didn't think too hard about my uncertain future. My family seemed to have their lives all figured out. Lanna had taken a while, but she was quickly becoming one of California's most popular painters, and she had a whole string of small business owners who relied on her to get well-paid gigs among the rich and famous. Her husband was called the King of Art and would be right back to it in no time (with a more competent bodyguard at his side). Catherine knew exactly what she wanted to do, and in a few years she'd be one of the country's top forensic linguists and off saving the world just like Seth. Even my brother Ben, before he'd died, had had a plan. He'd been saving up the money he would need to start a self-sustaining business so he could get married and raise a family.

And I had no idea what to do. Never had. Since the beginning, I'd only ever been able to see what was right in front of me.

"Come on, Orion! You don't have to do this." The shout to my left brought me to a pause. "No, don't—" Something shattered.

My heart jumpstarting to a faster pace, I quickly crossed the small street and slipped into a little coffee shop that I wouldn't have even noticed if the woman's voice hadn't caught my attention.

As my eyes adjusted to the dimmer light, she kept going: "You broke it, you imbecile," she said loudly. "Now how am I supposed to make espresso?"

Two men stood right up against the counter in matching black t-shirts, while the young woman I'd heard had grabbed a broom and was sweeping up what looked like the remains of a white coffee cup on the floor. Behind her, an espresso machine dripped a steady stream of water and steam. Both men were armed, though they unsuccessfully tried to hide their guns beneath their shirts. Instinctively, I lowered my hand and clasped my own gun, just in case.

Sighing, the woman straightened up and rolled her eyes at the two men. She didn't look particularly worried, though there was some anxiety in her green eyes that she couldn't fully hide. "Ares, would you tell your stupidity-laden friend that if I can't sell coffee, I can't make payments?"

"That's not our problem," the man on the left said, his voice cold and deep. "Boss wants what's due."

Her straight-backed stance sank a little as she folded her arms. "Well I don't have it. I'm sorry. I'll pay double next month, I just—"

"That's not how this works," the man named Ares growled, and his hand shifted for his gun.

Time to intervene. "Hey!" I said from the doorway. "How about you leave the lady alone, huh?"

Both men turned to face me. Orion, on the right, looked completely bewildered by my sudden appearance, but the other—Ares—grinned with amusement. He was taller and bigger than me, but he looked slow, a little too bulky for close combat.

"This isn't your fight," the girl said, glancing between the two men nervously. "I'm fine."

I smiled. I was in desperate need of punching something, and these thugs had given me the perfect opportunity. "Time to go," I told them but readied my stance in case they attacked.

Orion was the first to react, lunging forward in an attempt to catch me off guard. I slipped to the side and gave him a shove, throwing him right into the doorframe behind me. Ares threw a punch that I dodged easily, and I reciprocated with a hit to his jaw that sent a satisfying jolt of pain through my wrist. He was solid, I'd give him that. Orion was more agile than I expected, and he suddenly grabbed me from behind and knocked me forward, but I grabbed Ares in turn and brought all three of us to the ground. An elbow to his face took care of Orion, but Ares was twisting around and had me by the shoulders before I could slip out of his reach.

His fist came quickly, bringing blackness with it.

I opened my eyes to a curtain of dark hair framing a face so full of concentration that I wondered what she could possibly find so interesting.

"Ah," she said, "you're awake. Finally."

I groaned, my head pounding with every heartbeat. Had I really just lost a fight so quickly?

"You deserve that," the young woman said, getting to her feet and disappearing from view.

I sat up slowly, flexing my aching wrist as I checked out what looked like a storage room with half-stocked wire shelves. The young woman was standing in the doorway with a clipboard in her hand, writing something down and completely ignoring me. If she'd brought me to the back and out of sight, I could only assume it meant I'd been unconscious longer than I thought. "How long was I—"

"Twenty minutes," she said without looking up. "And now you're awake, so you can leave. I'm closed."

You're welcome. Struggling to my feet, I took a moment to stretch out my neck and arms then crossed the little room to glance out into the rest of the shop. The men had gone, and nothing else seemed to be broken or damaged, so that was good. "Are you okay?" I asked her.

Her green eyes jumped up to mine, and the anger in them actually made me take a step back. And in the weirdest way, it was almost familiar.

"What?" I asked.

She took a deep breath that only intensified her glare. "Thanks to your little stunt," she said, "they're going to come back angry. Wanting more money than before. I didn't ask for your help and didn't want it. Now leave."

I didn't like the sound of that. "They'll be back?"

She held her arm out toward the door, her eyebrows lifted high. I could have sworn I'd seen her before, and the longer I stared at her the more I was sure I knew that glare. "Leave," she repeated. "Before you destroy something else."

"The cemetery," I said as my memory clicked into place. She was the one with the bouquet of roses that had ended up puncturing my arms when we collided. She had the same green Converse shoes and everything.

She tossed her clipboard onto an empty shelf then pushed my shoulders with surprising strength toward the door. "I'm not going to ask again," she said. "I'll call the cops if I have to."

I wasn't about to stick around when I obviously wasn't welcome, but I grabbed the doorframe when we reached the front and turned back to her. "You didn't call the police on God of War and his pal Bozo," I pointed out.

Though her eyes widened a little, she kept an impressive scowl as she gave me one last little shove to get me out onto the sidewalk. "The cops can't do anything about Ares and Orion," she admitted. "They haven't done anything illegal." That was debatable. "You, on the other hand…" And then she slammed the door shut, locking it behind her.

And I stood there, my head spinning and my feet refusing to move because never in my thirty-five years had I been so completely and thoroughly disliked, and I very much hated the feeling.

I wasn't entirely sure what brought me back to the coffee shop the next morning, but I got in line at eight and fervently hoped it wouldn't get me a cup of boiling water thrown in my face. The young owner hadn't forbidden me from coming back, but I had no doubt she wouldn't be happy to see me.

Half a second after meeting my gaze, she groaned and threw her sharpie at me, which I caught before it hit me in the eye. *Impressive aim.* "Why?" she grumbled, shaking her head. "Haven't you done enough damage?"

I wasn't used to people not liking me right off the bat, especially when I wasn't using my bodyguard persona. But I supposed our first meeting, though it had lasted all of a few seconds, hadn't given her the best first impression, and the second had only made it worse. Third time the charm?

"I wanted to apologize," I said, handing her the marker back. I glanced behind me to make sure I wasn't holding up a line, and then I gave her a sheepish smile that only deepened her scowl. *Huh.* "I didn't realize I would make things worse yesterday," I said. She didn't seem to be stressing over whatever payment she apparently owed, though. Either she exaggerated the consequences of me intervening, or they hadn't come back yet. Either way, I wanted to try to make it better.

She folded her arms, and after making sure the skinny kid who was making the orders was fine, she jerked her head for me to follow her to the corner of the store so no one could overhear us, I assumed. "I shouldn't have gotten mad at you," she admitted, though reluctantly. She wouldn't even look at me as she spoke. "Ares—the one who kicked your butt—makes me nervous, and I had to put that energy somewhere."

Though her commentary on the fight stung, I decided to ignore it. "Does he come here a lot?" I asked.

She was about to answer when she changed her mind, clamping her mouth shut. Her eyes strayed over to her employee and the few customers at the little tables around the lobby, and then she sighed. "I have to get back to work. You can go now."

Seriously? "Wait," I said as I followed her back to the counter.

"I have customers to serve and an espresso machine to fix," she replied brusquely. "I don't have time to deal with your weird sense of nobility. I don't know you. You don't know me. Go find some cat to pull out of a tree or something."

What was her problem? "I was just trying to help."

She turned so quickly that I nearly ran into her. Again. And she looked right into my eyes with a determination that almost made me smile. Almost. "Look," she said and poked her finger into my chest. "Like I said yesterday. I didn't ask for your help, and I don't want your help. So either buy some coffee and a donut, or get out of my shop."

I hadn't had someone talk to me like that since my military days eight years ago, and it weirdly felt good to be ordered around again. Even if she was a girl several years my junior. Adam was painfully polite, and Catherine hadn't told me what to do in years since Seth had broken her out of her selfish ways. Outside of Benny telling me which toy car I could play with, I didn't have anyone giving me orders, and I practically craved it. "Yes ma'am," I said and grinned at her. She didn't like that, which only made me smile more. "How about a decaf? And a bear claw."

She stared at me for a second as if I'd said something completely ridiculous, and then she let out an over-dramatic sigh and slipped around the counter. "4.25," she grumbled and held out her hand.

I pulled out a ten and handed it to her with a wink, knowing she would hate that almost as much as she apparently hated me. My teasing hadn't gotten a reaction like hers in years, since Lanna and Catherine had both learned that the easiest way to shut me up was to ignore me. I had to admit I kind of missed that annoyed look she gave me. "Keep the change," I said, and she rolled her eyes.

"Of course you'd say that," she replied and turned to get my food.

I quickly found a seat in the far corner with a view of the door. If the well-named Ares came back acting like his namesake, the Greek god of war, I would be ready to show him the door. And this time, I wouldn't let him win so easily.

The shop owner arrived just a moment after I sat down, and though she didn't look all too pleased that I was still there, she dropped the plate with my donut onto the table and poured me a cup of coffee. "Eat your heart out," she said before walking away.

"Hey!" I called, and though she froze, she didn't turn around. I asked my question anyway. "What's your name?"

She spun on her heel, with the coffee in her pot sloshing dangerously close to the spout as she did. "Why do you care?"

"Indie!" her employee shouted to her, waving her over.

I grinned as she grimaced. "Indie," I said, deciding the name fit her well. "Is it short for something?"

Clenching her teeth, she debated not telling me but seemed to realize I would just keep asking. At least she was perceptive. "Indiana," she said with a sigh.

"Like the state?"

"Like the professor," she replied and hurried back behind the counter to help her coworker, a bit of pink spotting her cheeks.

I watched her for a few minutes, and though she never once looked over at me, I had a feeling she was very aware of me sitting there. Especially because her employee kept glancing up and accidentally making eye contact with me, and one of the muttered comments he gave to his boss looked an awful lot like, "Are you going to make him leave, or what?"

I dearly wished I could see her response, not just because a part of me wondered that very question. Would she actually let me sit here when she so clearly didn't want to? Whatever she said in response, she no doubt had some great insult to offer me, and I couldn't help but laugh a little. I would stay out of her way as best I could, but I was determined to stick around in case Ares and his buddy came back to cause more trouble, especially considering I'd made it worse. At least according to her.

However, when my coffee turned cold and my donut was long gone, I started to realize it could easily be a long day. Yesterday the goons had been there around four in the afternoon, and it wasn't even ten yet. I needed something else to do, something to occupy me until I could actually be of some help to the contentious Miss Indiana. Luckily, I had a whole bunch of family members who had plenty to distract me.

Seth answered after only a couple of rings, though his greeting was drowned out by some impressive shouting in the background. "Hang on," he said, and I heard two doors close before the near bellowing disappeared. "Sorry about that, Matthew. Catherine's not too pleased with the movers."

"Does she have them quaking in their boots?" I asked. I could easily picture my little cousin taking a bunch of burly men to task for putting a wrinkle in one of her sweaters.

"I'm pretty sure a couple of them are crying," Seth replied with a chuckle. "Catherine's a force to be reckoned with."

I settled against the back of my chair, grateful for his easy conversation and lighthearted nature despite his occupation. He was good for my cousin, even if I didn't like how often he showed me my shortcomings. "I thought intimidation was your job."

"Trust me," he said, "she's so much worse. We'll be lucky if there's anyone left to actually get her stuff across the country. So what's up?"

"Any luck with Sanford?" His contacts had thus far come up short on finding the weasel who tried to double-cross Adam, and if someone like Seth Hastings couldn't find him, I didn't have a whole lot of hope. But I really needed to hear something good, or the days were just going to get longer and longer. Until I found Sanford and locked him and his cronies away, I wouldn't be able to rest easy.

Seth's tone shifted to a darker timbre, and I could almost imagine his face as he spoke. "The man's a ghost, Matt. For someone who could barely hold himself together, I'm amazed he's stayed so hidden. Either he's got someone bigger and badder helping him out, or the sniveling imp he showed you was a mask."

"I don't like either of those options," I said, frowning. "I hate knowing he's still out there. Other people could get hurt, and if I hadn't—"

"If you hadn't been there, Adam would have died, Matthew. And lost a small fortune. Don't sell yourself short."

Sighing, I rubbed a bit of tension from my neck with my free hand and wished I could believe him. "Still," I muttered, "I'll feel better once you and Catherine are here in California. Security at the hospital isn't exactly up to snuff."

"Flight lands in San Fran tonight," he assured me, "and I sent a couple plain clothes over a week ago. They're positive the hospital has had no unsavory visitors so far, unless you count that eccentric mother of yours."

My heart sank into my stomach as that thought settled on me. Seth had sent a couple of his men to the hospital, and I hadn't even noticed?

I really *was* losing my touch. "Oh, that's… Thanks."

"Hey, I gotta go. Sounds like Catherine's threatening to move everything herself to show them how it's done. Which means I'll have to move it all if I don't stop her. See you soon."

I sat with the phone still pressed to my ear, staring at the opposite wall and telling myself that Seth's men were highly trained and had learned how to blend in completely. Become invisible. My few years in the Army weren't anything close to the training they had. Still, not even suspecting anyone I passed in the halls made me feel more than a little incompetent, which stung. A lot. I had definitely made a good choice in turning my role as protector over to Seth.

"Apollo, nice to see you as always." Indiana's carefully neutral voice broke me from my thoughts, and I turned just as she stepped forward to greet a tall and overly groomed young man whose stance mirrored almost exactly the two from yesterday. Add to that the Greek mythology name, and I was pretty sure he was another of the thugs I was here to intercept. But I had to tread carefully, for Indiana's sake as well as mine.

"Boss wants the money," Apollo said. He didn't sound as gruff as his warmongering counterpart, but I had no doubt he had similar training and wouldn't go down easily. He'd also managed to come at a time when the shop was empty except for me, which had to be deliberate, though I didn't think he'd noticed me in my corner yet.

Though her employee had retreated to the back, Indiana held her ground surprisingly well. "You can tell your boss exactly what I told Ares yesterday. I don't have the money, but I'll pay it double next month. It's been a slow few weeks, and now Orion's gone and broken the espresso machine."

Apollo took a step closer to her. I rose to my feet, knocking my chair back a couple of inches so it scraped against the linoleum. Both of them turned toward me.

"Don't," Indiana said, pointing at me.

But Apollo's attention was already firmly fixed my way. Just like Ares, he seemed to fit his name impressively well, a musical quality to his words and a boyishness in his face that probably belied his age. "You're the moron who got in the way yesterday," he said. It wasn't a question.

Moron? I raised an eyebrow, wondering if that was really the best word he could come up with for me. It was more on the tame side than

I would have expected. "I might be. I'm a friend of Indiana's."

She replied immediately: "He's not my friend."

I pretended to be insulted. "Ouch."

"Stay out of this," she snapped, adding a name under her breath that was a lot more like what I expected from her buddy Apollo.

Apollo, it seemed, wasn't as quick to action as his friends, and he stood calmly assessing the situation with a logical air about him. He knew from yesterday's encounter that I wasn't scared of the potential pain, and I'd obviously taken an interest in the young shop owner. Taking me in for a moment, he turned back to Indiana and muttered a quick, "We'll be back, Fierro," before slipping out onto the street.

Indiana Fierro. What a great name.

"*You*," she snarled, crossing the store so quickly that I took an instinctive step back in alarm. Two massive thugs, no problem, but apparently I had no bravery when it came to a five foot four woman in green Converse shoes. At least when she surprised me with that level of feistiness. "You need to leave. Forever."

Something about her insistence really made me want to stay, and I couldn't help but smile as she tried very hard to keep intimidating me but came up short. Catherine was only a couple of inches taller than this girl, but my cousin had years of experience manipulating the people around her and knew how to scare people off if necessary. Miss Fierro obviously spent most of her life appeasing the people around her, not fighting them, and her ferocity only went so far.

"What if I buy another donut?" I asked.

Her jaw literally dropped. "You're insane."

And she brought out the worst in me, it seemed. "I like to call it eccentric," I said, wondering just how far I could push her before she snapped.

"I really will call the police if you don't leave."

I folded my arms, thoroughly amused and almost desperate to keep tormenting her, if only to have a little bit of my life not completely inundated with real drama. "And tell them what?" I asked. "That you're refusing to sell a man a donut? I'm pretty sure the cops will take my side."

She narrowed her eyes. "Funny."

"I think so." Her face said more than any words could, and I knew she'd reached her limit. Grinning, I moved for the door. "I'll leave," I assured her, "but only because you're out of bear claws. Not because you scare me." I might have added that last part for my own benefit.

As I stepped out onto the street, I found myself breathing a little easier. While I hadn't had to fight and prove I was better than yesterday, at least I had gotten rid of Indiana's harasser. Plus, Seth had men at the hospital, so I felt better about leaving Adam there until he was recovered enough to go back home to his family and top-of-the-line security system. All in all, the day wasn't a total loss. Yet. I could only hope no other Greek gods attempted to get money from a hole-in-the-wall coffee shop until tomorrow when I could return and send them packing, though I worried there was only so much I could do. If all three of them came together...

Better not to think about how quickly things could go wrong. My biggest problem at the moment was finding something to do until tomorrow. As I was quickly starting to realize, being jobless sucked.

Since I couldn't bring myself to go to Lanna and Adam's house like I usually did when I had free time, I took to wandering the streets again in the hopes of finding something that could occupy me. In a place as big as San Francisco, surely there was *something* I could do.

I walked for hours, block after block until my legs started to complain from the endless hills. I hadn't paid attention to where I went, and the only reason I stopped was because my stomach growled at me in complaint, forcing me to pause and take in my surroundings. *Huh.* I'd landed myself just a block from the office building where my dad's law firm had sat for decades. I didn't visit often—Dad and I hadn't gotten along for most of my life—but I'd been there enough that I could count the windows and know which was his office.

The light was still on.

I glanced at my watch. 8:30. Last I'd heard, he'd been working on a pretty gnarly case, and I had a feeling he'd spent many a late night in that office recently. Odds were he had forgotten to eat dinner, like he often did when working long hours. And while seeking advice from my father had never exactly been my thing, I desperately needed someone to talk to who wouldn't just smile and tell me everything would work out.

Before I could chicken out, I hurried into the closest restaurant and grabbed two dinners to go, and then I headed into the office to have a chat with dear old Dad.

He didn't notice me at first, though that wasn't surprising. When-ever he'd concentrated on a document, even at home, very little could interrupt him. He sat at his large desk in the same leather chair he'd had for the last twenty years or so, his reading glasses nearly to the tip of his nose and his eyebrows furrowed as he mouthed some of the words he read from a piece of paper in his hand. His desk, like always, was piled with stacks of folders and large books and half-empty coffee mugs. (Mom would have died of shame if she ever took the time to visit his office. She was the queen of organization, unlike her husband.) I had to admit, I kinda loved knowing he wasn't as perfect as the world thought.

Dad looked tired, but I had a feeling that was his default nowadays. He wasn't particularly old, but his life as a corporate lawyer had started taking it out of him. His dark brown hair had gone silver in the last few years. Wrinkles lined his eyes. His shoulders didn't sit as high as they used to. I had to wonder how long he would keep working himself to the bone like this, since he didn't need the money. Was it passion for the work that kept him going, or was it something else?

He looked up when I sat in one of the hard-backed chairs on the other side of his desk and plopped a bag of food in front of him. "Mat-thew?" he said, and his eyes flicked to the clock that hung on the pale grey wall to his left. "Oh, when did…"

I smiled. "Stacy said you've been here since six this morning," I said, curious if Dad knew how dutiful his secretary really was. I had my suspicions she often worked as late as he did and was the reason he hadn't wasted away from starvation before now. She'd seemed grateful when I showed up and had left almost the moment I stepped past her.

Dad waved away my comment as if it was no big deal, but to his credit he reached into the takeout bag and immediately started eating the burger I'd brought him. "Your mother would go into a tizzy if she knew I was eating something like this," he said in between bites.

"I won't tell her if you won't," I replied and ate a few fries from my own bag. She'd gotten better over the years, but Mom generally cared more about appearances than enjoying life. "How's the case going?"

He let out a sigh, which wasn't a good sign. Dad was nothing if not stoic, and this slip in decorum meant he really was tired. "Sometimes I start to rethink some of my decisions," he said softly, almost as if he weren't really saying it to me. "I've done what I can for the case, and that's going to have to do. How is Adam? Lanna says he's gaining strength."

In more ways than one. My thoughts strayed back to the conversation I'd had with him yesterday, reminding me why I'd come up to talk to my dad in the first place. "I'm resigning as Adam's bodyguard," I said, the words rushing out of me as if I thought I might be able to breathe easier once they were gone.

It didn't help.

My dad set his burger on its wrapper and looked at me across the desk over his glasses. He was a hard man to read, and his slight scowl could have meant any number of things. I hadn't needed my father's approval for twenty-five years, but I still sat there tense, waiting for him to tell me how disappointed he was like he often had when I was younger. "Is there a particular reason for this choice?" he asked, just as the silence was getting uncomfortable. "You've enjoyed your time working with Munroe Royalties, haven't you?" I didn't know how, but he seemed to understand my reasons without me answering. And his expression was sad.

Maybe coming here was a bad idea. "Of course I have," I said, uneasy as I shifted in my seat. "Adam's my best friend, and I'd be stupid not to realize how lucky I was to be able to work with him. But…"

He laced his fingers together and rested them on the desk. "But you're afraid," he surmised.

I badly wanted to argue and tell him he was absolutely wrong. I was Matthew Davenport. I wasn't afraid of anything. Anyone who knew me knew that. But instead, I nodded and tapped my fingers on the arm of my chair as I spoke. "I nearly got him killed, Dad. After what happened to Lanna, I can't…" I let out a sigh to match his earlier one. "The people around me keep getting hurt when it's my job to make sure that doesn't happen. Clearly I'm not cut out for this kind of work." The last time I tried, I woke up unconscious in the back room of a coffee shop with things apparently worse than they'd been before, and I hadn't fixed the problem yet. "What if next time something bad happens," I said, "I can't save the person I'm supposed to protect?"

I couldn't remember ever being so honest with him. Up until about six years ago, I'd done my best to avoid the man, since he was convinced I needed to straighten up, get my life together, act like the elite Davenport I was. Seeing the way my parents treated the people around them, I'd rebelled against their lifestyle until they finally cut me off from their money to try to hide the fact that they had a disappointment for a son. I didn't talk to them for years after that, and things were still tense at times. I still wasn't their idea of a perfect son, but at least they had learned to acknowledge me as family.

Talking to my dad like this felt like something I should have done long ago, and I wasn't even sharing the worst of my demons. Maybe someday, but not now. There were some things I wasn't sure I would ever be able to talk about. Luke had always been the one to listen, and now that he was gone…

Dad sat almost motionless as he watched me, and maybe he was thinking the same thing as me. We didn't talk about ourselves in my family. We were too wealthy and powerful and well-known to show weakness. After what felt like several minutes but was probably just a few seconds, he seemed to make a decision about something and slipped his glasses from his face, folding them carefully and setting them next to his computer. "This case," he said, and he touched a finger to the nearest file, which was absolutely massive. "It's not my usual clientele, and it's likely one I will lose, but do you know why I accepted it?"

From the little I knew about my dad's cases, I had my suspicions he was the sort of lawyer who didn't accept defeat as an option. He'd represented some of the most powerful businesses in the state, and he was well-known for his ability to save companies millions of dollars. Sometimes billions. Though he was generally a soft-spoken man, never quick to lose his temper or even insert his opinion without request, he put on a mask of utter confidence in the courtroom that almost always worked to his favor and earned him the right to be called one of the most respected lawyers in California. If he had taken on a case he knew he would lose, I couldn't imagine the reason why.

Smiling just a little, he nodded and said, "I took this case because I believe in the cause behind it. This company deserves my help more than most, and I will fight tooth and nail to earn them recompense for what has been done to them."

Dad had taught me very little growing up, since he was always here at the firm or in his home office, too busy to bother raising his children. But I had a feeling he was telling me about this case because there was some sort of lesson he thought I needed to learn. More out of curiosity than a desire to believe he could actually impart some wisdom, I asked, "What does this have to do with me?"

He smiled, the gesture warmer than I'd ever seen it. "You can't save everyone, Matthew," he said softly. "But neither can you give up trying. Sometimes you may be the only thing standing in the way of someone losing everything, and though it may cost you more than you think you can give, you have to stand your ground. We Davenports have been given a lot of gifts in our lives, and it's our duty to use them to protect the less fortunate. However we know how." His smile shifted into something sadder, and he looked like Ben would have if he'd been able to grow old. There was a kindness in him I'd never seen before, and I suddenly thought maybe I understood why he spent so many nights working late at the office. It wasn't to avoid going home to my mom. It wasn't because he valued his status as a reputed lawyer. He worked as hard as he did and sacrificed as much as he did because he felt like he had to, because people needed his help.

For the first time in my life, I felt like my father's son.

And I knew exactly what I had to do.

CHAPTER FOUR

"Decaf," I said before Indiana could shout at me. "And a bear claw."

The to-go cup in her hands quickly turned into a lump of crumpled paper, and I told myself to be wary of her fingers in the future. They would likely pose a problem if wrapped around my neck. "4.25," she practically growled. Even her employee Harper found her reaction amusing; I could see him laughing silently as he gently dumped milk into a latte at the end of the counter. At least I was winning *someone* over.

Three days in a row, I'd come to make sure the shop didn't receive any trouble. Three days in a row, one of the Greek goons had come only to take one look at me and leave. Though I wasn't nearly as frightening as Seth could be, their decision that I was too dangerous to mess with was enough to make me want to keep coming just for the confidence boost alone. Besides, Indiana served up a damn good donut.

I handed her a ten as always and told her, "Keep the change."

She said the words with me, rolling her eyes. "Yeah, I know." Though I'd kept away people she obviously didn't want coming around, she still didn't like me even a little. Even during my drunkard days, I could get the prickliest of people to like me eventually, and the challenge was proving frustrating. At the very least she could thank me for keeping the goons off her back.

I took my usual seat in the corner and stretched out my legs on the chair opposite me, settling in for my sojourn. By now I'd gotten used to the uncomfortable seat, but the boredom was the worst part. People watching could only get me so far, since the shop generally cleared of visitors after the first few hours of being open. I'd brought a book the day before, but I was smarter today and had thought up something infinitely more entertaining to pass the time until I was needed. I just had to wait for her to show up.

Less than thirty seconds after I sat down, Catherine stepped through the door looking more than a little confused about my choice of meeting place for breakfast. I was sure she'd expected something more akin to a five-star restaurant, and until she saw me wave from my corner, she looked about ready to turn right around and order her driver to take her across town to the rich side.

To her credit, she didn't wrinkle her nose at the stains on the tables or the sorry state of the walls that badly needed a new coat of paint. She just crossed the room and slipped into the seat next to mine, plopping her wildly expensive purse on the table in front of us. "Seth thinks they have a lead on the guy who shot Adam," she said by way of greeting.

Nice to see you too. "Wait," I replied, "Sanford, or the asshole who pulled the trigger?"

Catherine rolled her eyes. "Is that really the best you've got? I thought you were a soldier, not a preschool teacher. Where's that foul mouth I know and love?"

"Ha," I said. The woman sipping her tea a few tables away would likely faint of shock if I used any of the terms I'd learned while abroad. "So he might have found the shooter?"

"Maybe," Catherine replied, taking in the dilapidated shop with a keen eye. She likely saw the same neglect I did, though only I knew the reason Indiana hadn't put more money into the repairs. She likely didn't have any to spare. "Your sketch matched a few hits in the database, though the names 'Lefty' and 'Righty' didn't exactly help narrow the search. Why are we here, Matthew?"

I shrugged. "Helping out small businesses," I replied. It wasn't exactly a lie.

"Right." Unconvinced, Catherine locked her eyes on Indiana, who had paused halfway through bringing me my usual breakfast and had matched my cousin's examining stare. I wasn't sure why they both seemed to be sizing each other up, though.

Finally remembering what she was doing, Indiana crossed the last half of the store and set my bear claw in front of me. "Can, uh, can I get you anything?" she asked Catherine, a line wrinkling her forehead between her eyebrows.

Catherine flashed her most dazzling smile that was enough to make anyone hate her for being far too beautiful for her own good. When she first came to stay with us a few years ago, I had known that that natural beauty of hers would get her into trouble. If she hadn't already found a man as good as Seth, I would guess there would have been plenty of eager suitors giving me enough stress to cause an ulcer. Catherine was formidable, but her emotions were more delicate than she liked to think. Going through the woes and heartache of dating would have done her more harm than good.

"Can I get an espresso?" Catherine asked, sounding surprisingly calm considering she still watched Indiana with an odd, sizing up sort of gaze.

"Broken," Indiana replied, giving me a glance before pouring me my own coffee. What was *that* look supposed to mean?

As she craned her neck to see the machine in question, Catherine's eyes lit up. "Oh, that doesn't look too bad," she said. "I can probably fix it."

"You can?" Indie and I asked at the same time.

Catherine just laughed and slipped around Indiana. In less than twenty seconds, she had the machine open and Harper watching wide-eyed and probably drooling. And I couldn't hold back my grin when I looked back at Indiana and saw her complete bewilderment.

"Is she for real?" she asked, slowly lowering herself into the nearest chair.

I could well understand her confusion. From all outward appearances, Catherine was every bit the perfect princess she'd paraded around as for most of her teenage years. Once she met Seth, she dropped the persona but never quite lost the look. Someone with perfect nails and hair that had more than once been lauded as "a divine 'do to die for" by the tabloid websites wasn't exactly someone who was likely to stick her hands in a greasy espresso machine. I knew she was smart, but I hadn't realized her genius included mechanics.

"My cousin is always full of surprises," I said softly, pride in my smile as I watched Catherine at work.

"Your cousin?" Indiana repeated, sounding surprised and...happy? But that couldn't be right, because in the next breath, she groaned and said, "Now there are two of you?"

I rolled my eyes and leaned forward so she couldn't mistake my sincerity as I said, "Oh come on. You don't have to like me, but at least be nice to her. She's fixing your machine, after all." In fact, Catherine was already closing it up with a satisfied smile and gesturing for Harper to come test it out. Though he nearly dropped the cup he held, he managed to keep himself together long enough to demonstrate that the machine did, to my surprise, work perfectly.

Catherine practically bounced back to us. "All good!" she announced, a little too pleased with herself.

Without a word, Indiana stood and made her way back to the counter to see for herself.

"I have a feeling they don't teach espresso repair at MIT," I said, raising my eyebrow. "Where did you learn something like that?"

The twinkle in her eye added to the mischief in her grin. "You'd be surprised how lucrative selling contraband coffee can be in an all-girls boarding school."

Full of surprises indeed. "Why would you need to sell espresso?" I asked. "I thought Daddy gave you all the money you could want."

Catherine just winked and replied with a vague, "Who said I sold it for money?"

Well that was a whole thing in and of itself, and I was yet again extremely glad for Seth's influence on her. If I had had any responsibility over her back then, I highly doubted I would have survived her many antics. I lifted my coffee to my lips, thanking whatever higher power there was that I had gotten the chance to know the good side of Catherine Davenport instead of the wild one.

I could only imagine what a teenage girl could want if not money, but before I could ask, Catherine leaned in close and asked, "So what's the deal with you and emerald eyes over there?"

I choked, spewing coffee all over the table. "What?" I coughed, grabbing a napkin and dabbing lamely at the mess.

Unlike her high and mightiness, her mischief hadn't gone away, which could spell trouble for me. "You know," she said and waved toward the counter. "The black-haired beauty who was absolutely thrilled to see me sitting here with you."

"Your sarcasm is a bit thick, don't you think?"

Rolling her eyes, Catherine took my hand as if we were having some heart-to-heart and I needed the comfort. That was generally my job, and I didn't like being on the other side of it. Especially when she gave me such a look of pity that it made me feel like I was missing some simple concept that she would have to explain. "Don't tell me you come here for donuts."

"Hey, this is a good donut," I replied, though I had a hard time keeping my voice light. Catherine was smart, sometimes a little too smart, and I didn't want her getting involved in something that could potentially be dangerous. I'd gotten enough of my family hurt, and I wasn't about to add her to the list.

"I'm sure her smiles make it taste better," she said, and she sounded like she was talking to a toddler. In fact, I was pretty sure it was the same tone of voice she used whenever she talked to little Benny. *Spectacular.*

I had to get a better hold of the conversation before things got worse for me.

I waited until I was sure she wouldn't say anything else before I took another sip of coffee. And then I shook my head and said, "I'm not so sure you're thinking of the same person I am. I don't think Indiana has smiled at me even once since I met her."

Oh, that probably wasn't a good thing to say. Not when Catherine's eyes grew wide with excitement. "You *like* her!" she declared, a little too loudly for my taste. "And you *want* her to smile at you."

I wanted her to continue refraining from strangling me every time she saw me. "You're way off the mark there, Kitty. Let's get back to this lead on Adam's shooter." It was bad enough that we hadn't caught the guy yet, but yesterday I'd learned the press had gotten word of the incident and now the whole internet was throwing around conspiracy theories about what or who sent the New King of Art to the hospital. We needed to end this, and soon.

But Catherine couldn't be distracted, not even by the nickname she hated so much. "In all the time I've known you, Matthew Davenport, I've never seen you show an interest in a single person, and you can't say it's because you're good at hiding it. It's written all over that pretty face of yours. If I had known, I would have set you up with Seth's sister, Lissa, ages ago. This changes everything!"

"Stop," I said.

"No way. This is——"

I put my hand over her mouth, my eyes locked on the door. "Seriously," I whispered tensely. "Stop talking."

Ares was back, and so was Apollo.

They'd only taken one step inside, and though Ares glanced my way, his eyes lingering a little too long on Catherine for my taste, Apollo kept his focus on Indiana. He spoke low, too low for me to hear, and she offered a single nod without an expression on her face. Harper was slowly wiping the counter clean with a rag, but he looked nervous. Whatever Apollo was saying, he didn't like it. Then, before I could stand and approach them, Ares muttered something to his comrade and the pair of them left without another glance in my direction.

"What was that about?" Catherine asked.

I ignored my cousin and went straight for Indiana. "What did he say?" I asked her.

She wasn't nearly as combative as usual, her brow furrowed in worry and concentration.

"Indiana."

"Go home," she said, and the words sounded a bit too much like defeat. Taking a breath, she turned and disappeared into the back room.

I looked immediately to Harper, who didn't need me to ask the question again.

"He said their boss is getting impatient," Harper said, quietly enough that Indiana wouldn't hear him. "He said she'd better learn her place before things go bad."

I cursed under my breath. I thought I'd been helping, but really I was making things worse. Just like Indiana had said. That seemed to be the way things went for me lately. "I should go," I muttered, my stomach twisting as I thought about what could happen.

"Wait." Harper slipped around the counter so he could lean in a little closer. "Right before he left, Ares told Apollo they needed to change things up if they want their money. He said…" He squinted, trying to remember. "'We need to come back later, when the Joe isn't here.' That's what he said."

The Joe. They knew I was ex-military, which meant they were more observant than I'd given them credit. That presented a problem, especially if they looked any deeper into who I was. But it also meant my presence made them more cautious, which could turn things more in my favor.

"Those guys give me the creeps," Harper admitted, frowning at the door. "I don't know who they are, but they've been coming around for a long time. I know she won't admit it, but Indie likes having you around, and once I'm gone I—"

"Gone?" I repeated in alarm. "Where are you going?" Indiana was going to be on her own? Never mind the thugs—she could hardly handle the early morning rushes even *with* Harper taking half the load. If her shop was already struggling, it could only get worse if she was missing her only employee.

Harper shrugged, though I could tell he felt bad. "Summer semester," he muttered. "If I don't graduate next year, my parents will stop paying for it, and they don't have night classes in the summer."

I couldn't exactly fault the kid for trying to get an education, but I definitely didn't like the idea of Indiana being at the shop by herself. She wasn't some damsel in distress, but she also wasn't a match for a man like Ares, or even Apollo. Maybe I could have Lanna contact her catering clients and find a replacement who knew Jiu-Jitsu.

"Maybe you should work here, Matthew," Catherine said loudly, suddenly at my side and nearly triggering my reflex to attack.

"What?" Three voices spoke in unison: me, Harper, and Indiana, who poked her head out of the storage room in alarm.

I stared at Catherine, wondering if the stress of moving from Cambridge had left her brain a bit scrambled. "You want me to work at a coffee shop?"

Harper said, "No offense, man," at the same time Indiana emphatically replied, "Absolutely not," and I looked at the both of them feeling slightly offended that they immediately had so little faith in me. Not that I thought it was a good idea. At all. I could only imagine the ways things could go wrong.

"Yeah," I said and took a step toward the door, "that's not going to happen."

Catherine grabbed my arm. "Not that I'm saying I know exactly what's going on here," she said forcefully, "but I can piece everything together pretty easily. You"—she pointed at Indiana—"owe someone money, and you"—her finger moved to Harper—"are working on your degree and quitting, and you"—her finger turned to me and earned a scowl—"are going crazy without a job and obviously miss your days of private security, considering you've spent enough time here that a couple of ex-military guys are scared to be here when you're around. Did I miss anything?"

"Private security?" Indiana asked, and she couldn't completely mask the admiration from her voice. That, or it was skepticism. More likely the latter.

I kept my scowl on Catherine. "How could you possibly know all of that? You were on the other side of the room, and you've been here for all of ten minutes."

"I read your lips, genius," she replied.

"But how did you know they were—"

She scoffed. "Please. I think I've spent enough time around you and my soldier to know one when I see one." Then she turned her attention to Indiana. "You've told the cops, right?"

I already asked that question. "They can't do anything," Indiana said with a little shake of her head.

Catherine wasn't deterred. "I know someone who—"

"Nope," I said, grabbing her arm and practically dragging her from the shop. I waited until we were safely out of earshot on the sidewalk before I continued. "There is absolutely no reason to get Seth involved in this."

"But he can help," she argued.

I had no doubt that he could. That was the problem. "He'll only make things worse, Catherine. He's too big a name and too famous a face to get involved in something like this."

"But—"

"I've got this, Catherine." *I hope.* "You should get out of here in case those men come back. I think one of them might have recognized you."

Flipping her hair behind her shoulder, Catherine rolled her eyes but seemed willing to listen to me for once. "As if anyone would be stupid enough to go after me when I've got a man like Seth at my side," she said, but it didn't fully mask the fear in her eyes. She still hadn't completely recovered from her abduction three and a half years ago, and I wasn't sure if she ever would. I had no desire to put her through that nightmare again. She was right, though. If she ever got taken again, Seth would likely tear the country apart until he found her.

"Just be careful, Matt," she said then gave me a small salute as she went.

Yeah.

Indiana and Harper were deep in a whispered argument when I stepped back inside the shop, and though she had a rage burning in her eyes, the kid was grinning. I had a pretty good idea who was winning the fight. As soon as she saw me, Indiana huffed and grabbed a bin to start clearing the few dishes left by previous customers. Harper, I noticed, quickly slipped into the storage room.

"Are you okay?" I asked her, choosing to stay by the counter instead of following her around the shop. I didn't want her to think I was any more of a threat than she apparently saw me as.

"I'm fine," she said a little too quickly, but in the next second she dropped into a chair looking completely exhausted.

"Indiana."

"Indie," she corrected, glancing over at me.

"Indie." Slowly, I stepped across the room and settled in the chair opposite her. For the first time, I was actually glad I wasn't as intimidating as Seth, because I wanted this woman to trust me, not fear me. "Look, I'm not going to let those guys get to you."

Her hands behind her neck and her elbows on the table, she met my gaze and didn't even try to smile. "You can't work miracles," she said, though it almost sounded like she wished I could. That was encouraging, at least. "Did you really work private security?"

I nodded. "And before that I was in the military. I'm not just some random guy trying to be a hero. I know what I'm doing." *I think.* After the last couple of weeks, I was starting to doubt, but she didn't need to know that.

Indie sighed, glancing around the empty store and then to the doorway. "Okay," she said, almost too quietly to hear. "I'll admit, having you around has been nice. I don't know if Ares has ever been hit that hard, and it's fun to see him a little nervous. And Orion won't even come back. But Apollo..." Shaking her head, she turned her green eyes to me and frowned. "He's smart. And he takes his time. He won't make a move unless he knows he can win, and that makes him dangerous."

"Who are these people, Indie?" Their names couldn't be real, which meant they were part of something bigger. Whoever their boss was, it was someone I had to be careful about crossing. The more I knew, the better.

But she shook her head and traced her finger over a raised bump on the table that could have been glue that had been spilled there years ago. These tables were junk. "I'm not saying I like it," she said, "but Harper's right. I could use someone to replace him. I can't pay you much, but..."

Miss "I don't need any help" was actually asking if I would work for her? I was impressed. I didn't think anything could humble her enough to admit something like that, and yet she was handling it with poise and dignity. *Good for her.*

"I don't need the money," I told her. And for some reason I put my hand over hers, which brought her eyes back up to me. "I just want to help. However I can." I put on a frown, which immediately made her nervous and nearly ruined my plan to lighten the mood. I fought back my growing smile, however, and with all the seriousness I could muster, I added, "I'll warn you, though, I have no idea how to make coffee."

Her smile immediately brightened the room, exactly as I hoped it would. "Well, if I can teach a teenager to do it, you might have a chance. Slim chance." She got to her feet, her smile still warming her entire countenance. "I'm a ruthless boss," she warned.

"I can take it."

Her smile widened, bringing out a surprising dimple in her left cheek. *Huh.* I never would have guessed. "Don't be so sure," she replied. Halfway back to the counter, she paused and looked back. "I should, uh, probably figure out what your name is, though. I've just been calling you 'The Inconvenience' in my head."

I laughed. "That's actually not the first time I've been called that," I said.

"Why does that not surprise me?"

I rose and stepped forward, holding out my hand. "I'm Matthew," I said. "Davenport."

She froze, her smile dropping, and I mentally kicked myself for using my last name. I may not have been as famous as the ladies in my family, but that didn't mean I was completely unknown. Not in this part of the world. "Davenport," she repeated, staring up at me. "As in…"

"Yeah," I sighed.

Indie pointed to the door. "So that was…?"

"My delightful cousin Catherine," I confirmed.

"Private security. That was for…"

Grinning, I folded my arms and waited to see if she could finish this sentence. She couldn't. "For Adam Munroe, yeah. The King of Art himself."

"Holy crap." She fell into a chair again, clearly overwhelmed. I definitely shouldn't have mentioned my last name. "Now I'm just confused," she said softly. "Why would you ever want to help someone like me? I'm… I'm nothing. Nobody. Not worth your time."

"Don't sell yourself short," I replied, my voice a little rougher than I meant it to be. Why was it everyone seemed to think I saw myself above them? I'd spent my entire life trying to be normal, and yet my name had haunted me from the beginning. Lanna was lucky enough to escape it, though at this point maybe Munroe was worse, and Catherine used the name to her advantage. I just wanted to get away from it.

"Let's pretend my name is Smith," I said with a shrug. "Then maybe you'll stop staring at me like I'm some sort of royalty."

Her lips twitched. "Matt Smith," she muttered, looking at me from head to toe. "How do you feel about bow ties?"

"What?"

"Nothing. So do you really want to work here? It's not very exciting, and it's not exactly private security."

I was pretty sure she was half expecting me to change my mind, and despite her insecurities, I couldn't help but shrug and purse my lips, pretending to think about it. "I dunno. You make a good point there."

Fear sparked in her eyes, and I had to hold back my amusement again. "I mean, we have some awesome customers who come in every day, and it's not like there's a whole lot of dangerous things that happen."

"Your Greek friends kinda negate that argument," I said.

"You get free coffee," Indie continued, her voice rising in pitch. "And I'll even throw in a bear claw now and then."

"I don't know," I muttered, scratching my cheek.

"Okay, a free donut every day."

Time to let the poor girl breathe again. Lifting my eyebrows high, I exaggerated my response. "A free donut *every day*?"

She grabbed a mug from her bin and chucked it at me with some serious strength. "You're an idiot," she snapped.

I just laughed and spun the cup in my fingers. "Of course I'll stick around," I assured her. "You don't even have to give me donuts."

"Harper!" she shouted and shoved the dish bin into his hands when he appeared at the storage room door. "Show this idiot how to use the espresso machine before I kill him." She sent me an impressive glare then disappeared to the back.

I couldn't help but grin as she went.

It didn't take me long to figure out why Indie didn't have the money to pay her Greek friends. By noon, Harper and I had only helped half a dozen people, which wasn't nearly enough business to make a profit let alone anything extra, even with the busier mornings. That she could pay Harper at all was a miracle by itself, and I wondered how long she could possibly keep the shop going before she was completely bankrupt.

The location was half the problem. I'd only stumbled upon the shop because I was wandering the city aimlessly. The nearby buildings were all warehouses or empty, and there was little to no foot traffic in the area. Those who did come in, Harper knew their names, so they either really liked Indie's coffee, or they came back out of loyalty or pity. Some of them I suspected were for the second reason. I didn't have any background in business, but even I could tell Indie was in trouble.

"Do you ever handle the deposits?" I asked Harper as the pair of us went into the lobby to wipe down tables. Not that they needed it, but we needed something to do.

The kid glanced at the storage room where Indie had been for hours and shook his head. "Indie takes care of all of that," he said. "I've asked her about it, though."

I fruitlessly scrubbed at a coffee stain and waited for him to elaborate.

"She says we're fine, but she definitely doesn't like when I bring up finances."

She wouldn't, if things were as bad as I suspected. Someone as strong-willed and independent as Indie wouldn't want anyone to know if she was struggling to make ends meet. But knowing this information didn't help me figure out what I could do to make the situation better. It wasn't like I could just throw some money at her and solve all her problems, though I badly wished it could be that easy so I could get out of her hair. Even just asking her about her finances would hurt the tenuous trust she had in me and likely get me thrown out.

Then what good would I be? "Has it always been this slow?" I asked. Maybe if I could drive a little more business her direction...

Harper shrugged, leaning up against a table. "When I started back in high school, it was a lot different. There are a couple offices nearby, and we're the closest place to get coffee. But after…" I wondered what that hesitation hid and why he swallowed and changed his choice of words. "After the gods started coming around, I think customers were too nervous to come back."

Now I really disliked the guys. Demanding money was one thing, but driving away business was another. "How long have they been coming around then?" I asked.

"A couple of years."

"Any idea why?"

"Nope. But I'm glad you're here. Indie needs someone to look after her, even if she doesn't think so." Harper gave me a little smile, which I reciprocated. He was young, but he was a good kid. He'd get far in life if he kept caring about people like he did.

"Anything else I should know about the job?" I asked. *Or about your boss?* There was so much I didn't understand about Indie, and Harper was the only one who could give me any insights before it was just me and her. She certainly didn't talk to me enough to give me those insights herself.

Shrugging, Harper led the way back to the counter. "There's not much to it, really. Indie does all the ordering and picks up the donuts from a nearby bakery every morning. As long as you don't spill very much or make disgusting drinks like you did this morning, you should be good. And keep that glare of yours handy," he added, his ears burning red. "It'll probably help."

Yeah, I definitely liked the kid. "So what are you…" I stopped and fixed my gaze on the front door as Apollo stepped across the threshold.

Up close, he looked even younger, probably twenty-five at the most unless his face was deceptively young. But his grey eyes were sharp as they quickly assessed the state of the store before landing on me. Impressively, he kept his expression completely neutral as he stepped up to the counter.

I leaned onto my elbows on the counter, trying to look as casual as possible while keeping myself ready. While he didn't look like much of a fighter, I wasn't about to disregard Indie's warning about Apollo's careful approach to things. He likely wouldn't be easy to surprise, so I couldn't be either.

"What can I get for you?" I asked.

Apollo spent a moment sizing me up, and then he asked, "Where is Fierro?" He kept his voice so carefully controlled that it sounded like a piece of melody torn from a song.

I shrugged one shoulder, something I'd seen Seth do a million times. It seemed to work for him. "Indie's on her break," I said, hoping that using her nickname would make me seem more familiar to her and therefore not some random guy here for a short visit. I wasn't going anywhere, and I needed Apollo to know that. "But I'd be happy to help you with whatever you need."

Apollo's eyes slid to Harper behind me. "Get her."

"Don't bother the boss, Harper," I countered immediately, letting my voice drop a little lower. "I'm sure our friend needs to be on his way."

Apollo's eye twitched, the first sign of anger he'd shown so far. "You'd do well to stay out of things that don't concern you, *friend.*"

I made sure my smile was nothing but a warning. "That's exactly what I'm doing."

"Matthew," Harper muttered. I could feel his trepidation behind me, but I wasn't sure how to help him relax. If he was afraid, that meant I wasn't completely doing my job, and I needed these Greek thugs to know they had no power here. Most people like Apollo only succeeded in their line of work because they maintained fear in their targets, fear that pushed the victims to keep paying for protection or whatever else. But if I stood up to these Greeks and showed them that that fear was gone, there was a chance they would give up and move on.

Apollo lifted his head half an inch, looking down his nose at me. "Tell Fierro this is her last chance," he said. "I'll see you around…Matthew." The corner of his mouth twitched upward as he turned and left the shop.

Before I could even take a breath, Indie suddenly appeared at my side. "What did you just do?" she gasped, breathing hard as she watched Apollo pass the last window. "Matthew, what did you say to him?"

I showed him he can't intimidate us. My smug response died the second I turned and saw her face. Her red-rimmed eyes still stared out the window, her nose running a bit and her face slightly blotched with red. Had she been crying since she went in the back this morning? Worse, was she crying because of me? No matter the reason, anger flared in my chest as I straightened up.

"Matthew," she nearly begged, and almost immediately my anger broke into sympathy. "What did he say?"

I reached out and put my hand on her shoulder, trying to figure out how to help her. With Catherine and Lanna, all I had to do was tell a joke or find some way to make them smile, but I didn't know Indie. At all. And I had no idea what sort of thing could bring a smile to the face of Indiana Fierro. So far I'd only managed it once.

"He didn't say much," I said. "Just that this was your last chance. But don't worry, because I'm not going to let them bully you. I promise."

There was something very pulling about Indie's teary gaze, in the way she looked at me as if trying to see if there was any way I could be lying. She had an enormous amount of strength in her, but there was an innocence there in the green depth of her eyes that made it impossible for me to look away. She was so young, and to be dealing with something like this… Was she really willing to trust me when I only seemed to make her life harder? I hoped so. I couldn't imagine being anywhere but here at this moment, assuring her that nothing was going to happen to her.

I didn't know how long we stood there, but Indie finally blinked and let out a sigh that sounded like she could hardly bear the weight on her shoulders anymore. "You can go for the day if you want," she said, for once not ordering me to leave. "Harper, you too." I'd forgotten he was even standing there. "They won't come back today."

I followed Harper out of the shop a few minutes later but paused in the doorway, glancing back to see Indie looking around her shop as if memorizing every little detail.

CHAPTER FIVE

None of the Greek gods showed up the next day. Or the next. Indie hardly said a word to me except to tell me what to do, and even Harper wasn't sure how his boss felt about the lack of pressure from the thugs. She kept her expressions decidedly neutral and rarely made eye contact with me, which drove me crazy. I felt almost helpless with no way of knowing how to make her situation better. But at least the Greeks were gone, and all I had to focus on was the shop. However boring that might be.

Whenever I found myself without something to do, which happened a lot, I took to watching Indie.

With Harper and me to work behind the counter, she had started roving around the shop and talking to the customers, sitting with them and chatting as if nothing were wrong. She put on an impressive mask, and I highly doubted any of the regulars could even tell something was wrong as she smiled and laughed. I had to admire her ability to hide what she was really feeling, since I'd been doing that most of my life and knew how draining it could be. Indie had clearly had a lot of practice.

Around lunchtime on the third Greekless day, a couple of old ladies shuffled into the shop and went straight for a table by the window without pausing at the counter to place an order. I grabbed a menu and was about to head their way, but I stopped dead in my tracks when Indie caught sight of them and squealed with delight. I stood dumbstruck, my chest tight, and watched as she practically flew across the store and into the arms of the nearest woman.

"Maria!" she gasped, beaming. "Stella! What are you doing here?"

The lady with the hand-knitted blue sweater with a penguin design on front stood a few inches shorter than Indie, which made her tiny, but she seemed absolutely pleased by the reception and didn't mind being nearly knocked out of her chair. "Can't we come visit our favorite granddaughter?" Her accent surprised me, since she didn't look nearly as Italian as she sounded.

Indie fell into the second woman's embrace, hardly caring she got slightly lost in the folds of the woman's massive yellow scarf. "I'm not your granddaughter," she said, though she still grinned.

It was the first smile I'd seen in her eyes that didn't carry a load of sadness with it, and I couldn't move or look away. If I had known such a thing was possible, I would have tried a whole lot harder to get it out of her.

"Nonsense," said Scarfy and gestured for Indie to grab a third chair. "You will always be family, dear Indiana." Like her companion's, her accent carried the same bouncing rhythm and soft vowels of Italian. *Indiana Fierro*, I thought to myself. *She's Italian.* "We are going to Hawaii for a few days, and we thought we would stop by and see you on the way."

Grabbing both their hands, Indie sat there positively beaming as she looked back and forth between the two women. She looked so much younger suddenly, and I couldn't decide if it was just because she was next to two people who were probably at least seventy. I had my suspicions her stress tended to make her look older than she really was. "I'm so glad you did," she said. "I'm guessing you can't stay long?"

Penguin Sweater shook her head. "*Sfortunatamente*," she said. "But we couldn't pass San Francisco without our little Indie."

Indie looked ready to burst with happiness.

"Uh, are you okay, Matthew?"

I jumped, turning around to find Harper with two teacups in his hands as he stared at me with an expression that told me I'd been staring just a little too long. "Huh?"

His lips quirked up in a bit of a smile. "I don't think I've ever seen you stand still for more than a few seconds," he explained.

No point trying to argue against that. "I'm fine," I said, but my voice almost cracked. What was wrong with me? "I never realized Indie was Italian."

"She's not," Harper said, and his smile faded just a little. "They're not really her grandmas, but they treat her like they are."

The name Fierro was definitely Italian, but I decided against asking for more clarification. There was a lot I didn't know about Indie, but I figured it would be safer if I didn't try to pry into her life unless she was the one giving me the answers to my questions. She kept her life private from me for a reason, and I had no intention of forcing myself into it if she didn't want me there, even if I was almost desperate to learn more about her. Indiana Fierro was an enigma, and I wasn't sure if she would ever let me figure out her puzzle.

I wished she would.

"That's Stella," Harper said, pointing with a teacup to the woman with the penguin sweater. "Maria has the scarf. They used to come in all the time, but they moved back to Italy about a year ago. Here." He placed the teacups in my hands and looked ready to laugh. What was so funny? "Why don't you bring them their drinks?"

I'd really rather not, I thought to myself, but I had a feeling Harper wouldn't let me argue. For a skinny little kid of twenty-one, he had a strong backbone. Praying Indie wouldn't hate me for interrupting her reunion, I slowly made my way over to the table and fixed on my most charming smile. Maybe I couldn't convince Indie to like me, but I prided myself on my ability to win the hearts of the elderly. To most of them, I was an absolute delight.

"*Signore*," I said, placing the cups on the table and trying to ignore the fact that Indie's gaze had turned dangerously sharp. "Are we having a lovely morning? Is there anything I can get you?"

Stella's gaze glittered as she looked me over, wrinkles appearing around her eyes before she turned to Indie and softly said, "Who is this young man? He is very kind."

"*Lui è bello*," Maria added, though she didn't seem quite as pleased to see me as Stella. I didn't have Catherine's language skills, but I could guess the gist of it from the way Indie's eyes went wide just before she hid her face behind her hands. I had to resist letting the compliment go to my head, since I didn't know precisely what it meant.

"He's my new employee," Indie said, her words muffled.

"I'm Matthew," I added and held out my hand for the ladies to shake. "And you must be Maria and Stella. Indie's told me so much about you, but I have to say you are more beautiful than she described."

Appearing from behind her hands, Indie looked like she was about to tell me off for lying. Luckily, Stella let out a happy Italian exclamation and patted my cheek. "*Ragazzo adorabile*," she said. "You are sweet."

"And he has work to do," Indie growled.

"Let him sit a moment," Maria insisted and waved toward another chair. "I would like to know him."

As I sat opposite her, I smirked at Indie and was pleased to see a bit of defiance burst to life behind her eyes, accompanied by a smile she fought to keep down. This was good. If I could get her mind off the shop, even for just a little bit, she might find some of the strength she needed to keep fighting.

"How long have you been with Indie, Matthew?" Maria asked me then took a sip of her tea.

"*Working* with Indie," Indie corrected under her breath.

I flashed her a wink then put my hand on Maria's arm. "Not long enough," I said brightly. "I wish I'd met her years ago."

"That would not have worked," Stella said.

I turned to her, and I had to bite my lip to keep from laughing. From close up, the penguin on her sweater looked awful, its head misshapen and a bunch of the stitches uneven. I loved it. "Oh?" I asked. "Why not?"

Flashing Maria a mischievous smile, Stella reached for her own tea and, after she took a drawn-out sip that was most likely deliberately slow, said, "Well, because of—"

"Because I didn't need any more employees then," Indie snapped, but she didn't sound angry. She sounded nervous. What was she hiding from me? And why was it making her turn so red in the face?

"And do you like making coffee?" Maria asked, apparently oblivious to her pseudo-granddaughter's distress.

I fought back another laugh. "To be honest," I said, "I'm not very good at it. But I like—"

"He likes annoying me," Indie said and sent an impressive glare my way.

Maria gave me her first smile since I arrived, as if she'd only just decided to start liking me. Stella, on the other hand, clapped her hands then patted both my cheeks this time. "You are a good boy," she said happily. "Good for our Indie."

"And handsome," Maria added, suddenly a little sheepish. She sank into her large scarf a little more. "*Molto bello.*"

Ah, *bello* meant handsome. Apparently she found me so handsome that she had to say it three times in two different languages. This time I couldn't help but laugh, and I leaned forward and kissed the old woman's cheek while Indie watched with horror. "And you are *molto bella*, Maria. I'm very glad I met you." Figuring it was safer to get out of Indie's death glare before it cost me my life, I gave Stella a matching kiss and told her how much I liked her sweater, and then I hurried back to rejoin Harper.

The ladies had watched me depart, but as soon as I was behind the counter, they launched into rapid Italian that Indie either couldn't understand or chose to ignore, because she just sat there with an expression of utter embarrassment. I didn't mean to add to her stress levels, but it was surprisingly fun to knock her off balance with something as innocent as charming my way into the good favors of her relatives.

From the look on his face, Harper was either impressed or concerned for my wellbeing. "I've never seen Maria smile at anyone but Indie," he said after a moment, and he shook his head as he watched me.

I felt happier than I'd been in a long time, and it wasn't because of Maria's infatuation. There was hope for Indie. Even if things were hard and likely to get worse, she wasn't so far gone that she couldn't smile, which meant there was still a chance I could save her.

The old Italians stayed for a couple of hours, and when they left, they both had smiles and waves for me before they said their goodbyes to Indie at the door. I was cleaning tables too far away to hear anything they said, but I could have sworn I saw Maria mutter, "*Molto bello*," one more time before they disappeared through the door.

When she closed the door behind them, I expected Indie to come get angry with me like she often did, but she took one look at me and just sighed, all of her burden returning to her shoulders, and I had the horrifying feeling that while she was glad to see her grandmothers, it had only reminded her of how bad things were for the shop and how little she had to be happy about.

"Harper," she said when she turned away from me, "I need to run a couple of errands, but I'll be back in a little bit. Will you be okay?"

Harper glanced at me in concern, but he nodded. Apparently Indie didn't often leave the shop during business hours. "We'll be fine," he told her and watched her head outside. "I think something's wrong," he said immediately after the door closed behind her.

What isn't? I thought and took a deep breath. Since I got here, things seemed to have only gone downhill, and there was nothing I could do about it. Everything I tried only made it all worse. "Do you think it's the shop?" I asked quietly.

He shrugged. "Maybe I shouldn't go," he said.

Maybe I couldn't help Indie, but I wasn't about to let this kid throw away his education. "How about you shut that thought down really quick," I muttered and scowled at him when he looked over at me. "There's no way I'm letting you postpone graduating just because of this little setback, whatever it is. I'll take care of Indie." I hoped.

Harper still didn't look convinced, and he wiped at a table that didn't really need cleaning. "But—"

"Don't finish that sentence," I said. "Your future is just as important as hers." And, since he grimaced and left the whole shop feeling dark and gloomy, I added, "What are you studying, anyway?"

Thankfully, he brightened a little. "Business," he said. "You wouldn't think I would like working in a place like this as much as I do, but I'd love to start up my own shop someday. I'm not as smart as Indie, though. She does it without a degree, no problem."

No degree, huh? Given her young age and experience in running the shop, I should have guessed as much, but it still surprised me a bit to know she ran this place without any formal training. "How long has she owned this place?"

Harper's expression was not what I expected, and I had absolutely no idea why that question would bring near anguish into his face. What was the cause of that pain in his eyes? "She's been here a little bit longer than I have," he said quietly and moved over to the counter to clean the already sparkling machines, which was a pretty clear indicator that he didn't want this conversation to keep going.

I, however, desperately wanted to know everything there was to know about this mysterious coffee shop owner. I'd never been so intrigued by someone in my life, and it was driving me crazy not having any answers to my ever-growing list of questions.

Indie returned twenty minutes later with balloons and some ice cream, apparently throwing an impromptu going-away party for Harper before he quit for his semester.

"I know it's not much," she said as she came through the door, her cheeks pink, "but I wanted to thank you for sticking with me for so long."

Though he smiled, Harper threw another glance at me that was easy to read; he was planning on coming back at the end of the semester, but Indie evidently didn't think that was going to happen. That wasn't a good sign. "It's perfect," Harper told her and gave her a hug. "I've loved every minute of working here."

Though the pair of them set up their little party on one of the lobby tables, I kept behind the counter. Indie definitely didn't want me in her shop any more than she had that first day, and I had probably pushed my luck by interacting with Stella and Maria as much as I had. I knew she only kept me around out of necessity, which wasn't my favorite way to be thought of, but I would take what I could get.

"Come on, Matt," Harper said, waving me over.

I looked to Indie, who took several seconds adjusting the balloon ribbon before she looked up at me. From this far away, it was hard to read her expression, but she jerked her head and shrugged. *Alright then.*

Instead of sitting, since the only seat nearby was right next to Indie, I leaned up against a table and took the bowl of ice cream Harper handed me. "The place will be much duller without you," I told the kid, and he actually blushed a little. "Though it'll be nice not to have you breathing down my neck every time I make a latte," I added.

Laughing, Harper shook his head. "You're terrible at it," he argued. "What do you expect me to do?"

"I can't help if my sister stole all the artistic genius in the family," I replied. "The girls got all the talent, and we boys got the looks."

Indie coughed suddenly, and it almost sounded like she was covering a laugh. So close; I'd have to try a little harder to get a smile out of her, apparently. I didn't have quite the same familial qualifications as her grandmothers.

"It's too bad your cousin couldn't stop by one more time," Harper said and immediately turned bright red.

I grinned, surprised he hadn't brought Catherine up before now. That must have taken a great deal of self-restraint. Or maybe he was just too intimidated to say anything. "Oh, I wouldn't go down that road if I were you," I warned him. "If you think *I'm* scary, wait until you see her boyfriend."

Again with the choking sound from Indie, though she didn't look up from her bowl.

Harper wilted a little, but only for a moment. He was smart enough to know he wouldn't have had a chance anyway. Catherine was leagues above nearly everyone, even upstanding guys like Harper. He kept his smile, which meant he'd be okay. "I'm gonna grab my phone," he said and jumped up. "We need a picture to commemorate."

The instant he was in the back room, I turned on Indie. "What's so funny, Indiana?"

Turning even redder than Harper had, Indie stared at me with wide eyes for a whole three seconds before she managed to recover with another cough and lifted her shoulders noncommittally. "I wasn't laughing," she said a little too innocently.

Sure she wasn't. "What, you don't think I'm scary?"

"You're about as terrifying as a terrier."

"Hey," I complained. "You say that like it's a bad thing. Terriers are scrappy, not to mention the cutest things on the planet."

She snorted, and for a second I completely lost my bearings as she fought against her laughter, though I had no idea what had caught my attention. Her smile wasn't all that different from the one she'd given Stella and Maria, but maybe that alone was enough to catch me off guard. I hadn't thought *I* could coax one of those smiles out of her on my own so easily. She really did look years younger when she smiled, and I wondered just how old she really was, though it wasn't exactly something I could ask her. Maybe Harper knew.

"You?" she asked once she swallowed her amusement. "Cute?"

I didn't think I'd ever wanted someone to say yes to that question more than I did in that moment. I'd never really cared before. "Your grandmothers think I'm beautiful," I said and tried to smirk, though it felt like I didn't do the job properly.

Indie rolled her eyes. "They think any man with a sharp jawline is beautiful. Don't forget, I've seen you passed out on the floor with drool coming out of your mouth thanks to Ares."

"Selfie!" Harper said, jumping between us with his phone in hand and holding it out to take the photo. Just as he readied his finger to touch the button, I glanced at Indie in the camera and caught a sadness that had suddenly slipped into her expression. I turned my head to look at her in the same instant Harper snapped the picture, but he didn't feel the need to take another.

By the time the kid moved back to his chair to finish his ice cream, Indie had plastered on a smile I didn't buy for a second.

"Indie, this was amazing. Thank you for everything." Harper pulled Indie into a tight hug, threw me a wave and a smile, and then he was gone.

And to my surprise, Indie spoke to me: "I'm gonna seriously miss that guy," she said. She looked tired but not as beaten down as she sometimes did, which was a welcome improvement, but she didn't bother hiding her sadness like she had during our little party. She even let a tear slip down her cheek as she stood in the doorway and watched him go.

"He's a good one," I agreed quietly. I needed to wipe down the tables and sweep the lobby, but for some reason I wanted to know what someone like Indie Fierro would say about a scrawny college kid who was way too grown up for his age. That seemed to be the theme of the shop, if I was right about Indie's age: too weighed down by grown up problems. It didn't hurt to smile now and then, or God forbid let out a laugh or two.

"Did you know he started when he was sixteen?" she asked, glancing over at me. I shook my head. "When my... When we hired him, I was sure he'd last a week before he gave up and went to a grocery store or something instead. But he never even called in sick. Five years he's worked here, and he's been such a good friend through it all." So Indie had been here for a little over five years, according to Harper. That wasn't long.

I took a wary couple of steps closer. Not because I couldn't hear her, but because it felt a little strange being nearly on the other side of the store. "He cares about you," I said. "Not a lot of people can say that about their employees."

"Trust me," she replied heavily, "I am well aware of that." And then she sent me a playful grin that knocked me to a standstill. Teasing? "And now I'm stuck with..." Her eyes travelled down to my toes and back to my face. "That."

"*That?*" I gasped, putting a hand over my heart. "I'm offended. First you call me a dog, now I'm just *that*." Insulting myself had gotten a few smiles out of her before, so I figured that was my best option for cheering her up, even if it meant cutting my ego a bit more than it already had been. "I mean, I may not be one of the cutest things on the planet, but—"

"Please," she said with another snorting laugh like earlier. "You're

Matthew Davenport. You're basically perf…" Her eyes went enormously wide, which gave me a great view of how green they really were. Most green eyes were greenish blue or hazel, but hers were *green*. Fresh summer lawn green.

My feet pulled me closer without my permission, slipping around tables until I was nearly at the door where she still stood. With her face flushed as red as it was, I couldn't keep myself from grinning. "Perfect, huh?" I asked softly. She was entirely wrong, but that didn't mean it wasn't fun to hear.

"I said basically," she mumbled, but there was a smile still playing at the corner of her lips. "Just don't let it get to your head. It's big enough already."

I wondered if Seth's signature half-shrug worked in situations like this, and I decided to try it. "That's sort of a family hazard," I said, "so I can't make any promises. But I'll do my best." Another step got me close enough that I could reach out and touch her cheek to feel how warm it was, though I kept my hands deep in my pockets. That wasn't exactly something I should be doing given our situation, and I doubted she'd be cool with it anyway. Touching Indie would likely get me slapped, though I wouldn't put it past her to throw a mean left hook either. There was so much I didn't know about this girl, but that didn't make me care any less about what happened to her.

My phone started playing "Colors of the Wind," and both of us jumped. Taking a couple of steps back, I smiled and answered the call. "Hey, sis," I said. "What's up?"

Indie slipped away to the back, and I furrowed my eyebrows. What had I done this time?

"*What's up?*" Lanna repeated, her voice full of annoyance. "I haven't seen you or talked to you in over a week, Matthew Lewis Davenport, and all you can say is 'What's up'?"

Well this was new. I hadn't seen her this angry since the first time she saw me after I got sober, and she'd given me quite the slap in the face on top of her furious words. Sitting on the nearest table and glad she wasn't near enough to slap me again, I took a deep breath before I answered. "Is something wrong, Lanna?"

"What's wrong is my brother quits a job he loves with no warning and just disappears without a word. Where have you been?"

Huh. I could have sworn I told Lanna what I was up to, but maybe I'd been too focused on figuring out who the Greeks were and how to stop them that I hadn't considered the fact that I hadn't been away from my family for more than a couple of days in at least three years. I hadn't gone a day without at least talking to my sister, so no wonder Lanna was worried. How was it I could mess up so badly in literally *every* part of my life?

I had to cover my tracks as best I could and try to make amends, though that part wasn't going to be easy. "Lanna, take a deep breath. I'm perfectly fine. And I saw Catherine just a few days ago. She knows what's going on."

"I'm not Catherine, Matthew, I'm your sister. Where are you? Obviously not home, since I'm sitting on your couch and you're very much not here."

"You're at my house?" Even *I* was rarely at my house, since I usually spent my time with Lanna and Adam. Besides, the last couple of nights, I'd booked a hotel room near the coffee shop just in case I needed to get there quick in case of a Greek invasion. Hopefully I hadn't been too much of a bachelor and left the house a mess. Knowing me, I didn't like my chances of that being true. I'd never been big on cleaning up my own spaces.

"Yes, I am at your house," Lanna said, "and I will be at your house until you get here and tell me what's going on with you."

Well that was an order if I ever heard one. She sounded a bit like our mother, and that was terrifying. "I'll be there soon, Lanna. I just have to…" I paused, turning toward the storage room when I caught movement out of the corner of my eye.

With a small smile, Indie gave me a wave then started sweeping, leaving little room for argument.

"I'll be there in a few minutes," I finished. "Maybe you could do some laundry while you wait."

"There is no way I'm touching your nasty clothes, Matthew."

"Dishes, then. See you soon."

I was about to say goodbye to Indie, but she'd put in earbuds, the universal sign of not wanting to talk. I just hoped that wouldn't last longer than today, or the next little while would get incredibly boring. As much as I loved standing around an empty coffee shop in silence for hours on end… There was no way I would survive if I had to sit still for that long.

The first thing to greet me when I stepped through my front door was three feet of toddler smashing directly into my legs and grabbing on tight. "Benny!" I said, reaching down and lifting him into my arms. I regretted ignoring my family as much as I had, but I especially regretted ignoring my nephew. His toothy grin brought warmth back into my chest and made me realize how much I needed my family in my life. "What are you up to, bud?"

"Really, Matthew?" Lanna asked loudly from the kitchen. I could practically hear her rolling her eyes, and I grinned. Mom *hated* eye rolling, and Lanna had taken to doing it as often as possible just to annoy her. "Is that the only question you know now?"

"Nice to see you too, sis."

With Benny sitting happily in my arms, I passed the little hallway leading from the front room to the kitchen. Mine wasn't a big house, something my mother complained about frequently, but I didn't need the space I already had let alone anything more. With Lanna and Adam happily settled in the huge Munroe mansion now that his dad had retired to Florida, and Catherine now renting out a downtown condo nearly the same square footage as my house, it wasn't like I even needed the house to begin with. Their homes were always open and infinitely more comfortable, and mine sat in a perpetual stillness I couldn't stand. I kept it mostly in case I needed to retreat.

Lanna was, in fact, doing the few dishes I had left in the sink the last time I stayed here.

"That was a joke, you know," I pointed out.

"I know," she replied. Which meant she'd needed the distraction.

Oops. *I* used to be the distraction, and I'd let her down by keeping my distance. What a terrible brother I was.

Frowning, I set Benny on the counter and handed him an old magazine, which would keep him occupied for at least a few minutes as he pretended to read it. "How's Adam?" I asked. He'd been released from the hospital a few days earlier, but I hadn't gone to see him yet. Our last conversation hadn't exactly been a good one, and I couldn't bear the thought of him trying so hard to convince me to come back to work for him.

Pausing in her scrubbing, Lanna sighed. "He's healing."

"But?"

"But it's really bothering him that something like this even happened."

I knew exactly how he felt, but this wasn't a conversation I wanted to have. I already knew it was my fault.

When she looked up at me, tears hung in the bottom of her eyes, which meant she was about to say something I absolutely didn't want to hear. "It's like Luke all over again," she said, making my stomach drop. "We should have seen this coming."

My friend had died protecting Lanna from a man who wanted to hurt Adam, something none of us had thought would happen. I had had my worries, but we'd never *really* considered Lanna a target until it was too late. If I had just listened to what my gut was telling me, maybe Luke wouldn't have…

Swallowing, I stuffed my hands into my pockets before Lanna noticed my fingers shaking. "Can we not talk about this?" I said. It was hard enough to talk about Ben, who had been gone for almost two decades. Luke had died less than six years ago.

Thankfully, my sister seemed to want to talk about him as much as I did, and she nodded before glancing around my sparse kitchen. After a moment, she let out another sigh, this one much more exaggerated. "This place is so cold, Matthew," she said. "You could at least put up a painting or something."

I smiled with relief. Leave it to my sister to point out how little I felt the need to decorate. Maybe if I actually spent time in my own house, I would put a little more effort in, but it wasn't like I had anyone to impress. "Give me one of your paintings, and I'll happily put it on the wall," I said. She was one of California's best, after all.

Though she blushed a little at that answer, she still eyed my bare walls as if they said a lot more than I thought they did. I wasn't sure I wanted to have *this* conversation either. "Doesn't it bother you not having any color in here?" she asked as she turned back to the sink.

I shrugged. "It's not like I'm ever here long enough to notice."

Pulling out the last plate and drying it off with a towel, Lanna put it with my other three plates then turned back to me with questions in her eyes. "So where are you if not here?" she asked. "Where have you been?"

Now we were getting to the fun stuff. "I, uh, I got a job," I said. More or less.

"You *had* a job."

"Ha!"

Lanna didn't like that answer, and her scowl was admittedly impressive. She was generally so even-tempered, just like Adam. "What's that supposed to mean?" she asked. "You don't think working for Adam was worthwhile?"

"It's not the job I was questioning." Ah crap, that wasn't what I was supposed to say. I didn't need my own sister confirming what I thought of myself when my own criticism was painful enough.

Lanna pulled her eyebrows together, leaning against the counter and watching me with eyes that saw too much. When had she gone from my innocent baby sister to someone who probably understood exactly what thoughts plagued me? It was supposed to go the other way around. "Matthew," she started.

"You don't have to say anything," I said and bent to help my nephew turn the page of his magazine so I didn't have to look at her. "I know I messed up."

"That's not what I was going to say."

"Sure it was. All this stress that's eating away at you is because I couldn't keep your husband safe. Trust me, I'm well aware of that."

"Don't put words in my mouth, Matthew."

"The internet has already done that for me," I muttered. "You know they agree with me, right? That it's my fault the King of Art nearly died?" All my searching for Sanford had given me plenty of time to read through the comments people were leaving about the incident. About me.

Lanna huffed. "People on the internet are idiots," she said. "I don't blame you."

"Exactly." Then I paused, looking up at her and trying to understand. "Wait, you don't?" That didn't make any sense. "But you said it was my fault."

She frowned. "I never said that."

"On the plane to Boston. You said—"

"I said I didn't want you to beat yourself up over something you couldn't control."

Taking a step back, I tried to remember the conversation. Sure, she'd been half asleep, but she had spoken pretty clearly from what I could recall. "You said Seth was better at finding Sanford so I shouldn't even try."

Her expression turning sour, Lanna crossed the kitchen so she stood right in front of me. "There you go putting words in my mouth again," she said and rolled her eyes. "Yes, I said Seth is better at finding people. That's his *job*, Matt, and he has the whole military to back him up. But I didn't say you should give up. I only meant you didn't have to do it all on your own." She lifted a hand and put it on my shoulder, and her eyes trailed over the whole of me. "You look tired," she said. "I worry about you being all alone all day."

And now she pitied me. *Awesome.* So maybe I had read into her sleepily mumbled comments on the plane, but that didn't mean any of the tension had left my shoulders. I worried where this conversation would go if I didn't tread carefully. I was already exhausted from keeping Indie's spirits up without making her hate me more than she already did, and I cared about Lanna a whole lot more. If I had to brighten her day too, it was going to make for a very long afternoon. "I'm not alone all day," I said, as if I hadn't heard her comment about how tired I looked. "I have a job, remember?"

One concerned conversation wasn't about to stop me from trying to take care of the people around me, no matter how hard Lanna tried.

"Right." She grabbed Benny from the counter just before he reached out for her, and she frowned at me as if trying to glean information just by looking at my face. "Catherine said something about a coffee shop, but she was a little all over the place settling in after her move. Coffee? Really? You don't even like coffee."

I would do best to lie and keep my real reasons for working with Indie a secret. The last thing I needed was to add to Lanna's stress. "I happen to be good at making it," I told her, though according to Harper that wasn't necessarily true. "And the hours are good." *Though I don't think I'll actually get paid, but that's beside the point.* I wasn't sure if Lanna was convinced yet, so I added, "And it's only temporary, until I figure out what I should do with my life."

"Hmm." Lanna narrowed her eyes, searching for more, but I refused to say anything else about the subject. It was bad enough that Catherine knew the truth, but at least she hadn't told Lanna the real reason I was at the shop. "Well," she said finally, "maybe don't mention that last part to your date tonight. Women don't particularly like unambitious men, in general."

I definitely heard that wrong. "My what?" I said.

"Your date."

"I don't have a date." I hadn't had a date in years, and my last had been an absolute disaster. It still gave me nightmares.

Lanna laughed, hoisting a suddenly sleepy Benny over to her other arm. "Sure you do," she said, "even if you don't know it yet."

What was that supposed to mean? "Lanna."

Digging into her pocket, Lanna grabbed a slip of paper and held it out to me. "Catherine has set you up with one of her friends who happens to be here in the city for a few weeks. She and I both think it's about time you started looking for a partner in crime."

The paper had an address and the name "Cecelia," which wasn't exactly a lot to go on. My chest constricted as I stared at it. "Lanna, there's a reason I don't date," I said and felt a slight tremor in my voice. *Awesome.*

She laughed again as if I'd said some hilarious joke. "Don't be stupid. You date all the time."

"No. I don't." Dates were awkward and full of pressure, and inevitably I ended up making a fool of myself without meaning to. I was no Adam Munroe, who only had to smile to melt the hardest of hearts. And I certainly wasn't Seth, who had half the country in love with him without even trying. Ben had been the handsome Davenport brother, and I had learned early on to accept that I was meant to be on my own. Dating was for people who actually had their lives together.

"Catherine says Cecelia will be there waiting at seven," Lanna warned, her grin far too amused to make the situation anything but worse. "I'd hate for her to be waiting for nothing."

Dang, Catherine knew what she was doing. "You two are the worst," I grumbled.

Lanna just nodded smugly and headed for the door. "Have fun tonight!"

I stood in the doorway until she drove off, trying to figure out how I'd suddenly lost control over my own life. But if I was being honest with myself, I had probably never had it to begin with.

CHAPTER SIX

I realized too late that my wardrobe primarily consisted of dark t-shirts and suit jackets. Spending the last several years as a bodyguard had taught me to stay subdued and impressive, and my closet had almost completely transformed. What did normal people wear on dates? Certainly not something quite so ominous as my usual attire. Still, Lanna had barely left me enough time to shower let alone stop by the store and find something better, so I settled on my lightest blue shirt and a pair of dark jeans, with a grey jacket over the top. It wasn't great, but it was the best I had. Perhaps I should have gotten dressed when Lanna was still around so she could tell me I would do better to not show up at all rather than show up looking like a guy who had no idea what he was doing with his life. That look, however, was probably unavoidable, since I had no idea what I was doing with my life.

I didn't know what this Cecelia person was expecting, but I hoped I didn't completely disappoint. It wasn't like I had anything exciting to offer, but I *was* Matthew Davenport. We Davenports were born and bred to be impressive, and I wasn't about to shy away from a challenge.

Even if it terrified me. I could go up against thugs and confront my uncle and march into hostile territory no problem, but put me in front of a woman and expect me to act normal? *Ha.* There was a reason I was still single.

I arrived at the appointed restaurant at almost exactly seven. If not for the fact that this Cecelia person was apparently waiting for me, I wouldn't have come at all, but the girls had backed me into a corner, knowing I would never leave her hanging. My family knew me too well.

I paused just outside the door, taking deep, calming breaths that only made my nerves worse. Seriously, what was wrong with me? I had no fear of guns or fights with men bigger than me, but the idea of sitting down and forcing one on one conversation with a complete stranger... Honestly, if Lanna had called it anything other than a date, I would have been fine.

"Time to make an idiot of myself," I muttered then pushed through the door before I could change my mind.

The hostess offered me a smile of greeting, but it was the woman in front of her who caught my attention. Tall, slender, and absolutely perfect, she flashed me a well-practiced smile that set my gut churning. With that fancy dress of hers, she absolutely had to be (and she made me feel completely underdressed). With every inch of her flawless and glittering, Cecelia was clearly an elite, part of the world I had tried for years to get away from. What was Catherine thinking? She had to know me better than that.

"Cecelia?" I asked, likely failing to make my smile look at least a little real.

Cecelia had no such problems and only smiled wider. "You must be Matthew," she said in a voice dripping with superiority.

Must be. As if she didn't already know everything there was to know about me and my family. I held out my hand. "Nice to meet you," I said. *In a manner of speaking.* I glanced at the hostess, suddenly unsure if Catherine had made a reservation or if we even needed one. It was a fancier restaurant, but it had been so long since I even went out to eat at a place like this that I honestly didn't know what I was expected to do.

Reading my expression and taking pity on me, the hostess smiled and said, "I have your table right this way, Mr. Davenport."

I didn't know if tipping a hostess was a thing, but I planned to find out and give her a large one. "Thank you," I breathed and followed her into the lion's den.

I recognized many of the people seated around the overly gaudy restaurant, though not by name. My mom would know every single one of them, which likely meant they all knew me. That would definitely explain the many disappointed looks they not-so-discreetly sent my way. I certainly didn't look the part of an elite and rarely had since Ben died. For the last seventeen years, I'd done everything I could to be nothing like them, and for the first time, it bothered me that they cared. Couldn't they just concern themselves with their own lives and let me live mine in peace?

"Will this be okay, Mr. Davenport?" the hostess asked, holding out her arm to a table slightly hidden by some fake trees. Blessed girl was getting the biggest tip of her life.

"This is perfect," I said, even though Cecelia didn't seem to like the idea of not being seen by the whole room. She would get over it, assuming she managed to get over herself. "Thank you."

I pulled Cecelia's chair out for her then took my own seat, breathing in deep and searching for the strength to make it through the evening. Unless Cecelia miraculously happened to be more than what I saw on the surface, I was going to kill Catherine for putting me through this.

"Do you have a favorite wine?" I asked before our waiter arrived. "I'm not much of a drinker myself."

Cecelia pulled the corners of her mouth up in what I assumed was supposed to be a smile but looked more like a grimace. "A Sauvignon is fine," she said carefully, most definitely to judge my reaction.

I may not have looked like an elite, but I'd certainly spent half my life as one. Giving her a half smile, I cocked my head and said, "White, huh? I took you for more of a rosé person," waiting for her anger to rise. No one in this room would even think of going for a pink wine.

Amazingly, Cecelia managed more of a smile. "I guess we'll just have to get to know each other better then."

So my comment had won me some points, had it? *Interesting.* "So tell me, Cecelia,". I said. "Are you from the Bay Area, or do you know Catherine from the East Coast?"

"Dear Catherine and I met in Paris, actually," she replied and spoke both name and city with a French accent. *Cute.* "We were both attending a fashion show and became chères amies."

Dear friends? I was starting to doubt that connection had continued after Catherine's transformation into who she was now. I was starting to doubt a lot of things about this woman sitting in front of me, and I was pretty sure there was nothing about her that wasn't completely artificial, including her interest in me.

"So what brings you to California then?" I asked, sitting as casually as I could manage.

Cecelia didn't appreciate my slouch, not bothering to hide the disgust in her expression as she eyed me. "I'm visiting friends," she said, "and I *was* hoping to make some new acquaintances."

I grinned. "And now?"

"We'll see."

Ah, so I still had a chance. *Excellent.* "So what do you do with your time, Cecelia?" I asked. If she said anything along the lines of shopping or attending parties, I wasn't sure I would last much longer. I wondered what the record was for the world's shortest date; there was a high chance I would break it if things kept up this way.

"I run a nonprofit helping bring school supplies and lunches to kids in Africa," she said. "We do a lot of work with the Alvarez Trust."

I sat up straight. The Alvarez Trust was the most prolific charity organization in the city. Even after avoiding the world of money as long as I had, I knew that working with them was an impressive feat. "Wait, really?" I asked.

She smiled, the first real smile I'd seen so far. "You sound surprised."

"I am," I admitted.

"Not all of us waste our money on useless pursuits, Matthew," she replied, sounding a little like she was scolding me.

"Yeah, I deserve that," I muttered and found myself smiling. So maybe she wasn't completely awful. "How long have you been doing that?"

We talked about her organization well into our meal, and I quickly found myself enjoying the conversation. I even thought I might almost like Cecelia, who definitely had a passion for her work and seemed to truly care about the kids she helped. After an hour, I'd nearly forgotten how horribly the date had started.

"You're going to have to forgive me," I said, knowing she fully deserved an apology. "I didn't come into this with the best mindset, and it may have skewed my perception of you. I'm sincerely sorry."

Cecelia's smile was alluring, definitely one of her best features, though she had many to contend. "You thought I was just a vapid woman focused solely on her looks, didn't you?" *Guilty.* "You of all people should know you can't judge a book by his cover, Matthew."

Ouch. Insult and chastisement all in one. My mother would definitely like this girl. Which was a little terrifying, considering my mother and I rarely saw eye to eye. "You've set me straight," I said with a grin. Maybe Catherine wasn't crazy after all, and I actually didn't want the evening to end. Who would have thought? "If you're finished," I said, "maybe you'd like to go—Indie!"

I jumped to my feet just as Indie passed by our table, my face suddenly burning. But why would it matter if she saw me on a date? She didn't even like me.

Muttering something to the older woman who was with her and waving her onward, Indie glanced at Cecelia then gave me a somewhat strained smile. "Fancy seeing you here," she said, trying and failing to go for a light tone. Was she still having a rough time dealing with everything at the shop? She didn't look like she'd been crying. Much. Then again, it had only been a few hours since I'd seen her, so she had no reason to be in a better mood. This seemed like a deeper sadness, though. Whatever it was.

"I, uh…" Because *that* was coherent. "How are you? It's good to see you." I sounded ridiculous, and heat blazed even hotter in my face as I stood there trying not to make *more* of a fool of myself. I didn't have any problem talking to her at the shop, so why was it suddenly impossible to speak like a normal adult human? *Get it together, man.*

Her smile turned a little more genuine, though she looked absolutely uncomfortable as she strangled the strap of her purse with both hands. "You saw me just a few hours ago, idiot."

I clamped my jaw shut, glaring at her a little but more amused than anything. She certainly knew how to put a man in his place, and her comment eased the tension I felt between us until it almost felt like we were standing behind the counter of the shop and about to launch into a conversation where she insulted me and I did everything I could to make her smile. Why I should be more comfortable when insults were impending, I had no idea.

She looked nice, I realized, a little more dressed up than usual and her dark hair curled prettily, which made sense given the location. But if she couldn't afford to run her own store, how did she afford to eat at places like this?

Cecelia coughed behind me, and I remembered it wasn't just the pair of us standing in an empty restaurant.

"Sorry," I said quickly, noticing several pairs of eyes on us around the restaurant. "Indie, this is my… This is Cecelia. Cecelia, this is Indie. My…" Why was it suddenly so hard to think of words again?

"His boss," Indie finished and held out her hand. "Nice to meet you."

"Oh." Cecelia suddenly straightened up to an absurd degree and put on her best high-class expression of disapproval. "So you're in private security too?"

Indie must have found something funny, because she could hardly hold back her laughter as she shook her head. "I'm in coffee," she said simply, and my stomach twisted. "See you in the morning, Matthew."

I couldn't even manage a mumbled reply as she left. This was going to be fun.

"Coffee?" Cecelia repeated, using the word to pull my attention back to her. "As in importing?"

Might as well get this over with. "As in serving," I replied, sinking back into my chair. "Indie owns a coffee shop downtown."

"Why would a coffee shop need security?"

Oh, the night just kept getting better. I couldn't help it; I laughed, drawing half a dozen more gazes our way and bringing a blush to the poor woman's cheeks. She would enjoy my response: "Oh, Cecelia," I said. "I'm so sorry, but you've certainly gotten the wrong idea about me. I don't do security. Not anymore. I make coffee, pure and simple."

The redness in her face darkened, blotched by bits of paleness no amount of makeup could conceal. "You make coffee," she repeated, almost whispering. "I don't understand. You're Matthew Davenport."

And at the moment I desperately wished I could be anyone else. Clearly my name never worked in my favor when it came to dating. How could it when I had never truly lived up to it? "Up until a few days ago I was unemployed," I told her, grinning like the idiot she would inevitably think I was. "And now I work in a shop that's probably going bankrupt."

She couldn't even fake a smile anymore. "But your parents—"

"Disowned me when I was seventeen," I said. She didn't need to know they had since returned me to their good favor.

"So you're..." Cecelia couldn't even find a word for it, and she sat there for a moment as her brain processed this information. And then, right as I was about to suggest we end our unfortunate date and part ways forever, she got to her feet with a dazzling smile. "I just realized I have somewhere very important to be," she said and stepped toward the door. But she paused and looked down her nose as me. "You know," she said, "I didn't want to believe everything I'd read about you, but clearly my first instinct was right. I knew I shouldn't have come." Then she turned quickly and marched off, leaving me sitting alone with a restaurant full of judging eyes pointed right at me.

Yeah, I was *definitely* going to kill Catherine.

"Matthew!" Catherine stood at her door with much too big a grin for my taste. "I see I succeeded."

"Succeeded at what?" I grumbled, stepping past her and into the living room of her new condo. "Reminding me why I don't date the upper class?" *Or at all.* I plopped onto her couch without invitation, letting the stress of the whole evening slip away. At least now I knew not to trust Catherine's opinion if I ever decided to try again.

The jury was still out on if I would.

Catherine settled next to me, still a bit too pleased but at least mildly sympathetic. "Was she really that bad?"

Yes. Yes she was. Beneath the admittedly surprising charitable occupation was a woman who didn't care about who I was, just what I had to offer. "The second she found out I work at a coffee shop," I said, "your *chère amie* up and left. So yeah. She was that bad."

Sighing, Catherine pulled her legs up onto the cushion beside her and put on a thoughtful face. "First off," she said, "I wouldn't call Cecelia my friend. Not after she cozied up with Leo when he clearly promised to take *me* to his movie premiere. Don't ask," she muttered when she saw the question in my eyes. "Second, do you really think she was after your money?"

I shrugged, dropping my head back and closing my eyes. "My money or my name. I checked on my way over; her little organization is running low on funds, and Miss Cecelia and her salary are probably at the heart of the problem."

"Hmm."

I opened my eyes. "Hmm? Is that really all you have to say for yourself?"

Pushing some hair behind her ear, Catherine opened her mouth to make some sort of excuse, but I didn't let her say a word. I grabbed her left wrist, my heart suddenly spasming in my chest as I stared at the alarmingly large diamond sitting on her finger. That hadn't been there a few days ago.

"Catherine," I said slowly, "please tell me there's nothing on your finger and that I'm just hallucinating because it's been a long day."

But her grin said everything. "I was going to call you after your date," she said through her smile.

My grip tightened. "Where is he?" I growled. I was going to kill him. Seth Hastings had wasted his last breath on four little words.

"Matthew."

"Tell me where he is, Catherine. Is he here?"

She, apparently, didn't think my anger was real, and she laughed, pulling her wrist free. "No, he's not here."

Well that wasn't any better. "Why not? He just proposes then runs away? What kind of man is he?"

"I'm confused," Catherine said as I stood and took to pacing the room.

Seth should be here. With Catherine. Unless he was off keeping Adam safe, there wasn't anywhere else he should be except protecting her. There were Greek thugs who recognized her and knew her connection to me, and Seth just left her here on her own? Where the hell was he?

Catherine furrowed her brow as she watched me pace. "Are you mad that he proposed or mad that he's not here? Why are you mad in the first place?"

I paused, shaking my head. There wasn't exactly an easy answer to her question, and I didn't fully understand my reaction either. There was no one on the planet who could be better for Catherine and no one I would trust more to keep her safe and happy. Seth was, on all accounts, perfect. And I had no need to question whether Catherine *was* happy, because I knew beyond a doubt that she was. And I wasn't worried for her safety. Not really. So why was I angry?

Catherine held out her hand, and I slowly crossed back to the couch and joined her again. "What's wrong, Matthew?" she asked. "I know he didn't ask your permission, but..."

I shook my head. "I'm not stupid enough to think of you as someone who needs permission to make her own choices, especially ones as easy as this one. And I'm not your father, so I—"

Grabbing both my hands, Catherine smiled and held them tight. "Maybe not," she said, "but you've looked after me so much more than he ever has. You're every bit my brother as Lanna is my sister."

I sighed, brushing my hand over her hair. "I know that."

"So what's wrong? Is it because I'm too young?"

Twenty-one was hardly young, especially considering she had already graduated from MIT and was well on her way to running the country. "You and I both know you've never acted your age," I said softly. "That's not… That's not the problem."

"So what is? I thought you'd be happy for me."

At the first sign of a tear in her eye, I broke, dropping my head and wishing I could have just started with a smile instead of freaking out like I had. But it had been a long day. A very long day. My reaction further evidence I was only good at making a mess of everything I touched. "Oh Catherine," I said, brushing the tear from her cheek and doing my very best to smile at her so she wouldn't keep crying. She deserved to be happy. "I'm sorry. Of course I'm happy for you. Thrilled. Even if it doesn't look like it."

She still wondered why I'd reacted the way I had, but now that my thoughts were settling, I wasn't sure I had the heart to tell her. She was moving on. Getting married. In a few months she would have a husband who never left her side, and she wouldn't need me anymore. Just like Lanna didn't need me anymore. Adam was better off without me, and I only seemed to make things worse for Indie every time I tried to help. Seth proposing to Catherine left me with no one to look after, and I'd never felt so completely, absolutely useless.

CHAPTER SEVEN

When I woke the next morning, I had the worst hangover of my life. This was particularly annoying because the last time I'd had even a sip of alcohol had been nearly seven years ago, before I sobered up and got my life back together, so it wasn't even a real hangover. I was still perfectly sober, but the tiny bit of dim light that shone through the blinds of my bedroom seemed to sear right into my head, determined to let me know just how poorly I'd slept last night.

I dreamed about Adam. The day he was shot. It replayed through my head over and over again, and no matter what I did, the outcome was always the same. I watched my best friend fall time and time again, and I knew it was completely my fault and there was nothing I could do to go back and change things.

I could tell without moving I would be sore for the next several days from thrashing around in my bed like I always did when plagued by nightmares. I used to dream about Afghanistan all the time, and though I didn't dream about my time in the Army much anymore, those nightmares always left me slightly off kilter unless I found something to distract me, and fast. Unfortunately, my best alternative was not much better.

I couldn't be mad at Seth for proposing to Catherine, though he wasn't helping the dizziness that swarmed around me as I sat up. He and Catherine had been together for more than three years, but if I had known he was thinking so seriously, maybe I would have...

"Don't lie to yourself," I mumbled out loud, mostly to fill the silence of my empty house. Letting go of Catherine would have been hard no matter when Seth took her from us. I highly doubted they would go very far, but she wouldn't be my baby cousin anymore. She really had moved on.

I showered slowly, letting the cold water wake me up and counter the headache that probably wouldn't go away anytime soon. I knew I was being ridiculous. Catherine was a grown woman and could make her own decisions. But that didn't make things any easier, and I figured it would take more than a dying coffee shop to stop me thinking about how unnecessary I was becoming in the lives of my family.

As I dressed in just a t-shirt and jeans—no point in trying to be fancy after that disaster of a date last night—my phone buzzed on my nightstand and pulled me back toward the bed, where I was tempted to flop and take a ten-minute nap. But I resisted. Reluctantly. And I grabbed the phone and slipped on my shoes as the text opened with a picture from Harper.

It was the selfie he'd taken yesterday while we had his goodbye party. I glanced at the message he'd sent along with it—"Take care of her"—before bringing the picture to full screen so I could really look at it. As usual, Harper grinned wide, and he didn't seem to have noticed he was the only one who actually looked happy. Indie's smile was just as forced as it had looked at the time, which was why I was looking at her instead of the camera. But now that I wasn't trying to see past Harper's arm to get a good view of her, that smile looked even worse.

She was hurting. Bad. If I had been suspicious that she was losing the coffee shop, I was practically certain of it now, because that look in her eyes was one I knew well. I had seen it in the mirror for years, the look of someone who had lost almost everything and wasn't sure she had the strength to keep going.

I had to help her. Even if she didn't want me there, there was no way I was going to abandon her. She didn't deserve to be dealing with everything alone, and I would do everything I could to help her through it.

I just wish I knew how.

When I stepped into the shop twenty minutes later, I expected Indie to have her mask on and make some joke about my date. Obviously she'd found something funny about the situation last night, and I braced myself with a forced smile for a witty remark or cutting insult. But as I pushed through the door, I did not expect to see Indie sitting at a table with one of the regular customers, biting back tears as she listened to what the woman had to say.

"Indie?" I asked in alarm.

She held up a hand, stopping me in my tracks. "Not now," she said.

I knew better than to contradict that order. Slipping a black apron over my head, I stepped behind the counter and started prepping the best I could while trying to catch even a hint of why she would already be having such a terrible day.

The customer—Peggy, I think her name was—unfortunately stood a moment later and patted Indie's hand. "You'll get stronger every year," she told her with a comforting smile then left the store.

I had to tread very carefully if I wanted to avoid pushing Indie to a breaking point. The last thing she needed was me making her fall apart. But I couldn't just stand there and wait for her to break the silence, not when we didn't have any other customers to take care of. Taking a deep breath, I peered over the counter as Indie continued to sit and stare at the wall.

"Indie?" I asked softly.

She blinked, turning her gaze to me. Oh boy, she looked even worse than a moment ago. *Take cautious steps, Matthew.* I wasn't afraid of people crying, but my usual method of comfort—taking her hand and/or pulling her into a tight hug—probably wasn't going to fly. I wasn't opposed to holding her, but more likely than not it would end up with her punching me in the gut.

I swallowed. "You okay?"

Blinking again, her eyes roamed the shop until they landed on me again. "I'm fine," she said, and if not for her completely miserable expression, I might have believed her. She sounded impressively calm and unmoved.

"Are..." This was a worrisome question, and I leaned on the counter to hide a little. Just in case. "Are you sure?"

She nodded once then rose, brushing a tear from her long lashes and taking a steadying breath. "How was your date last night?"

I stared at her as she came around the counter to join me. This was about my date? Those tears weren't... They weren't over me, were they? "It was..." *Fine.* "Awful."

The honesty sparked a tiny smile, nothing close enough to bring out her dimple but definitely an improvement over the impending tears. "Awful?" she asked, clearly hoping for more details. "But she was beautiful. And you seemed to enjoy your conversation before I interrupted."

"Yes, she was beautiful," I agreed, "but none of it was real. Nothing like…" I stopped myself, frowning. Had I really been about to say "nothing like you"? I could admit Indie was attractive, but it was in a more natural sort of way. She didn't have to try to be beautiful. "And she was buttering me up all of dinner," I continued, "trying to get her hands on my money."

Indie's smile very nearly grew as she straightened the donut display. "A gold digger, huh? I wouldn't have guessed she was low on cash."

"*She* isn't," I explained. "Her company is. And she's not likely to put any of her shopping money into it."

"So she was using you," Indie said, turning to face me. "And *I'm* using you."

"I'm kinda forcing you into that one," I said. I didn't want her to think I had any desire to leave, especially now that she might actually talk to me instead of making us work in awkward silence.

Shrugging, she took a step closer and leaned on the counter next to me. "Do you like being used, Matthew?"

Well that was a strange question, and I wasn't entirely sure how to answer. "I like being needed," I replied, and suddenly all the weight I felt from my conversation with Catherine returned all at once. *Ouch. Can we go back to talking about my failed date?* That was a much safer topic. We could laugh about how surprised I was that Cecelia didn't ask if I needed help paying for dinner, or discuss how underrated well-informed hostesses could be. We could even talk about how I wore a jacket and jeans to one of the city's fanciest restaurants.

But Indie kept quiet, choosing to wipe down the counters in silence until the morning rush started a few minutes later.

The rest of the day we hardly spoke, and if we did, it either regarded the shop or something equally trivial, like if I'd seen any good movies lately or if she thought it would rain in the next couple of days. The hours dragged on, and I spent most of our down time juggling coffee cups or on my phone looking for Sanford despite not having any new leads. The conspiracy forums were only getting more ridiculous as time went on, and it wasn't like Sanford had really left any clues behind in the first place.

The only time we had a conversation longer than ten seconds was when, in an effort to deep clean beneath the espresso machine, I bumped a cup with my elbow and knocked it from the counter. I nearly caught it, but it slipped through my wet fingers and shattered at my feet, the sound echoing across the empty shop.

Indie looked up from her laptop where she sat in the far corner, nothing but annoyance in her eyes. "Really?" she groaned, though by that point I was so used to her frustrated tone that it didn't quite have the effect she wanted it to.

I shrugged as I grabbed the broom to sweep up my mess. "Just trying to keep you on your toes," I said, cringing. I sounded ridiculous.

"If I wanted more broken cups, I would tell Orion to come back."

"Ouch." Making sure she saw me press a hand to my chest, I clicked my tongue a couple of times and approached her table, broom and all. She tended to be in better spirits when insulting me, so maybe this would improve the overall mood of the store. "Keep comparing me to a buffoon like that, and I might have to leave."

Her sigh brought me to a standstill. "Could you?" she said, though I could tell she immediately regretted saying that when her cheeks blushed a little pink. "Sorry," she muttered and turned her gaze back to her screen. She needed me as much as I needed something to do.

I just wasn't sure how long this could last.

Slipping back around the counter, I grabbed my phone again and resumed my search, though I had no idea where to look anymore and just stared at my screen, hoping for some stroke of luck or inspiration or divine intervention. Sanford was a ghost, and if I couldn't find a guy like him, what good was I?

"Who are you texting, by the way?"

I looked up, surprised to find Indie looking at me with a bit of a frown wrinkling her brow. "What?"

She nodded toward my phone. "I mean, it's not like I can get mad at you for not working when there's nothing to do. I'm just curious about who can keep your attention for so long. A girl?"

I chuckled and returned my phone to my pocket. "I'm looking for someone," I said, only realizing how that must have sounded when she raised an eyebrow. "Not like that. Dating is…it's not my thing. I'm looking for the man who hurt my brother-in-law." Only, she wasn't supposed to know anything about my failure, and I winced. I had to keep her thinking I could actually protect her, or she might kick me to the curb.

Getting up from her seat, Indie slowly approached me and cocked her head to the side. "Someone hurt your brother-in-law? Shouldn't the police be handling something like that?"

"Technically yes, but they've hit the same dead ends I have." I sighed. "I don't even know where to look anymore." Even going through every celebrity chat forum and reading every article about the event, I'd found nothing. Unless by some miracle Seth found a new lead, Sanford was going to get away with it. With that lovely thought running through my head, I slumped against the counter and closed my eyes. I was so tired. And it was more than just my nightmares last night. I was tired of the people I loved being targets. I was tired of not having the resources I needed to do what had to be done. I was tired of coming up short in every way.

"So you're just giving up?"

I looked up in alarm when I realized Indie sounded angry. She *was* angry, standing there and glaring at me like I'd just insulted her. "There's nothing else I can do," I said, knowing how lame that sounded but not having the energy to make it better.

And Indie seemed to think I was a lost cause. Letting out her breath in a huff, she looked me over once then made her way back to her computer, leaving me standing there wondering if there was anyone in the world I could avoid disappointing. "I thought you of all people would be persistent," she muttered, almost too quiet for me to hear. "Someone should be."

Basically, by the time Indie said she was fine to finish closing and I could go, I was completely miserable. With no sign of the Greek gods nearly all week, my need to be there was quickly turning into simply another body to make coffee for a failing store. Indie didn't want me there, anyway. Unless things picked up or Apollo and his friends made their move, I was going to have to find something else to occupy my time, and I had no idea what that might be. What did millionaire ex-soldiers with no real skills even do with their time? Aside from becoming Batman, of course.

When I pulled into the cemetery, I wasn't very surprised. Though I'd been planning to go home to my bare-boned house and heat up a frozen boxed dinner before going to bed early, my subconscious must have known I needed *someone* to talk to about my life. Lanna would only pity me, Catherine was way too happy with her new fiancé for me to burden her with my problems, and I had yet to see Adam since I quit, which meant my main confidant was the person I was avoiding the most. The only person I would have forever was the only person who couldn't leave because he was already six feet underground.

"Hey, Ben," I said, settling against my tree as the sun sank low in the sky. The days were getting longer, but night would still come soon and leave the cemetery peaceful and dark. "I know I've been coming here a lot lately, but I figured you wouldn't mind. You never did say no to a late-night chat when I needed it."

Ben had been the perfect brother. He took care of Lanna and kept her away from Mom's most criticizing moments, and he kept me out of trouble for the most part. Until he died, I'd never stopped to wonder if he ever took care of himself.

"You worked too hard, Ben," I sighed. "And even when you left, you were still trying so hard to please everyone. And I…" I didn't make it easy for him. "Every time I got in trouble at school you somehow made it go away so Mom and Dad never knew. I still don't know what you did or how you smoothed things over so many times. I should have been expelled more than once, and I should have…" I sighed. I should have thanked him. Or at least made it easier for him.

As the sun cast an orange glow over the cemetery, I took a deep breath and let it out slowly, trying to release some of my tension with it. It didn't work. "I don't even know how many times you told me I wasn't overlooked." I said. "You said over and over again I was just as important as anyone else, and I really wanted to believe you. I still do."

I just wasn't sure I could.

"You have to tell me what to do, Ben. I keep getting more and more lost, and my family's moving on without me. Can't you just…send me a sign or something? Give me some sort of direction so I don't end up spiraling like I did before. Tell…" I paused, movement catching my eye. "Indie?"

She was a decent distance away, but I could clearly see the bouquet of roses held tightly in her hands. Just like the last time I'd seen her here. Who was she visiting? Conversation with my brother could wait; I badly needed to solve this mystery.

Indie walked with a purpose, traveling a well-known path toward whose grave she was visiting. It surprised me that she wasn't concerned about the empty cemetery or the fact that the sun was quickly sinking and leaving the whole place in shadow. Personally, I didn't complain about that part because it gave me a chance to follow her without being noticed. Still, if I could follow her, so could Ares. They'd stopped coming to the shop, but that didn't mean they wouldn't try other methods.

I paused just behind a small mausoleum as Indie came to a halt in front of a tombstone standing relatively by itself. I could just make out the name Fierro etched into the granite, but that didn't tell me much. I'd have to get closer to see a name or a date, but even then I'd have no idea if it was a brother or her mom or something closer. I didn't know why that last option bothered me as much as it did.

"Hi, Dante," Indie said suddenly, and I leaned just a little closer to hear. "I know I'm a little late this year, but I couldn't leave the shop. Sorry." She crouched down, resting her roses next to an impressive display of a large variety of blooms. Those other flowers were fresh, so someone else had come to visit Dante today.

Standing straight, Indie folded her arms and took a long, deep breath. "I don't know if I can keep my promise," she said, and the pain in her voice nearly pulled me forward. But I stayed put, hoping to learn more before I left her to mourn in peace. "I'm trying," she said, "but I can't… I'm going to lose everything, and there's nothing I can do."

The shop. I was right, and she was losing the shop.

"Tell me what to do, Dante," she said, and her shoulders shook. "I don't know what to do anymore, and I just wish you were here so you could show me which way to go. Help me figure out my future. I'm just so lost."

She stood in silence for a while, likely crying over the grave of her undetermined loved one, and I couldn't help but share her pain as I watched her. I'd just barely said almost the exact same thing to Ben, but neither of us was going to get an answer. The dead didn't talk, no matter how much we wanted them to. One of these days we would have to realize that we—

I cursed as Indie turned, immediately catching my eye and leaping back in fright. "Sorry!" I said and held up my hands in surrender.

She stomped over to me so quickly that she actually backed me up against the tomb behind me before I even realized she was angry. "Are you following me, Davenport?" she spat and held up a little pink cylinder.

"Please don't use the pepper spray," I begged.

She didn't lower her hand. "Answer the question!"

"No, I wasn't following you." *Much.* "I came to talk to my brother." I pointed in Ben's general direction, though it wasn't like she could see his headstone from here. "You have to believe me, Indie." I had no desire to experience the burn of pepper spray again. The first time, a prank during my time in the military, had been bad enough, and that stuff was diluted. This was pure fear and righteous anger waiting to turn me blind with pain unless I could convince Indie I spoke the truth.

She hardly moved, though her eyebrows pulled together a little. "Your brother?" she asked.

I nodded. Vigorously. Oh jeez, did I still have my hands in the air like some mugging victim? *Just take my dignity and go.* "He died seventeen years ago, but I like talking to him when I need to think things through," I said. She *had* to understand that.

Way too slowly, Indie lowered her weapon hand as she tried to read my face. Hopefully she saw some honesty there and not just pathetic fear. "Sorry," she said after a moment. "You just scared me."

Now that the immediate threat was gone, I laughed a little and dropped my own hands to my sides. "I'm pretty sure I was the scared one in this situation," I said and rolled my eyes at myself. "How do you do that?"

She cocked her head. "Do what?"

I wasn't sure how to put it into words, certainly not ones that would help me look a little better. "Completely throw me off my game," I said. I didn't think I'd ever fully felt in control of my situation when I was around Indiana Fierro, and it was starting to drive me crazy.

Indie certainly took her time responding, but her reply wasn't at all what I hoped to hear: "Was he your older or younger brother?" Why couldn't she just talk about herself for once?

"Older," I said, trying to figure this girl out.

"How old were you when he died?"

I didn't want to talk about this. "Seventeen."

"You poor thing."

Okay, that was pushing things a little too far. Folding my arms, I turned the focus back on her. "Who were *you* visiting?"

She immediately turned pale. "Dante."

Seriously, what was with this girl and avoiding the topics I wanted to hear about most? "And Dante is your…?"

She swallowed, staring at the mausoleum wall next to me so she wouldn't have to look at me. "He's my husband."

My heart seemed to sink down to my stomach, though I had no idea why those few words hit me so hard in the gut. "Your husband,"

I repeated. "What happened to him?"

Brushing away a tear that slipped onto her cheek, she shook her head. "I should probably head home," she said and started walking toward the entrance to the cemetery, as if our conversation was over.

There was no way I was letting her get off that easily. Falling into step beside her, I tried to keep my voice soft so I wouldn't spook her into running. Talking to Indie was turning out to be much like approaching a stray dog. Sure, she was cute, but I had to coax her into sharing if I didn't want her to bite me in the—

"You don't have to follow me," she said, throwing me a scowl.

"You happen to be going where I'm going," I replied lightly. "This is the only way out, if you remember."

She groaned. "You're so ridiculous."

"Thank you."

"That wasn't a compliment."

"I know." We passed my Audi, and the only other car in the parking lot looked like it belonged to the cemetery staff. I paused for only a second. Where was Indie's car?

"Seriously," Indie said, "you can go home." Had she walked here? I'd never actually seen her with a car. How far did she live from the shop, anyway? Night was falling thick and fast, and this part of the city wasn't exactly a cheerful place.

I spoke slowly so Indie couldn't possibly misunderstand me. "You're insane if you think I'm going to let you walk home on your own. Pepper spray can only do you so much good."

"Well you're not giving me a ride," she said with a surprising amount of authority in her voice. She kept herself just a step ahead of me, and if I sped up, she did too.

I could have easily broken into a run and forced her to do the same, but I just smiled and maintained the short distance between us. "I wasn't going to suggest a ride," I said, wishing I could see her face.

She glanced back, her wide-eyed confusion almost funny enough to make me laugh. "So you're just going to keep following me?" she asked as if nothing in the world could be worse. Usually I had to work to get women to dislike me, but with Indie it came naturally to her. And that only made me want to try harder to get on her good side. There was so much I didn't know about this woman, so much I was determined to discover if she let me. She was like some puzzle I had to solve or I'd never sleep through the night again.

I shrugged, matching her steps. "If the idea of me following you is so terrible," I said, "you could always let me walk next to you."

Stopping at an intersection, Indie turned to face me and surprisingly didn't look up at me in anger. Just more of that bewilderment as she took me in. "I really don't understand you," she admitted. "Where did you even come from?"

Grinning, I replied, "Well, you see, when a man and a woman—"

"You're an idiot," she groaned and stepped into the street even before the crossing light changed to go.

Maybe I was an idiot, but that didn't make me enjoy teasing her any less. Hurrying to catch up, I fell into step beside her and said, "How about I answer one of your questions seriously, and you answer one of mine honestly? Sort of a trade."

She looked at me from the corner of her eye, probably trying to figure out how my suggestion could be a trick. How many people had betrayed her in the past to make her so closed off? Was it really so hard for her to trust someone? I'd been hanging around her shop for almost two weeks, and she still thought I might be after something.

"Why aren't you working security anymore?" she asked, turning her gaze to the sidewalk in front of her.

Right to the hard question, huh? The answer that first came to mind—*Because I've always wanted to make coffee*—I couldn't give thanks to my offer to be serious, but neither was I about to tell her that I was convinced I wasn't cut out for the job anymore and my own brother-in-law had nearly died thanks to my stupidity. At this point, she already knew more about the situation than I liked. I wanted an honest answer from her badly enough, though, that I was willing to really consider her question. But that made things difficult.

Taking a deep breath, I spoke slowly. "I started questioning what I should do with my life. Being a bodyguard didn't seem like the answer anymore." And now it was my turn. "What happened to Dante?" I asked. Or any of the million questions that went with that one.

Indie frowned, likely reconsidering her decision to go along with this. "He died," she said.

"Oh, come on!" I flipped around and started walking backward, keeping my eyes locked on hers. "A real answer, Indie."

She fixed me with a hard glare, but there was way too much going on inside that head of hers for it to be very effective. Her expression kept shifting—a twitch of her lips here and a crease of her forehead there—until I could see her resolve breaking. She was stubborn, but I had a feeling she was starting to realize I could be worse. I had spent my life fighting, whether on the playground or on the battlefield, and Indiana Fierro had not. I didn't need to know much about her past to know she was a lot gentler than she pretended to be.

Sighing, she finally nodded then said, "A couple of years ago he got sick. And he never got better."

Finally a little insight into the mystery that was Indie Fierro. She was grieving. And suddenly I felt like I understood her, because if anyone knew what it felt like to lose a loved one like that, I did. Multiple times. But before I got the chance to ask any follow up questions, my phone started playing "Eye of the Tiger." Anyone but my family, and I would have ignored it until later, but Seth never called. That had to mean it was important. Quickly apologizing to Indie, I turned back around to walk next to her as I answered the call.

"I got a lead on Sanford," Seth said before I could even say a word.

"You did? That's amazing!"

"Yeah. He's close, too. Look, I'm going to be without my phone for a few hours so he won't know I'm coming. Look after Catherine for me?"

"Of course," I replied immediately. "Good luck."

The line clicked dead without another word from my future cousin-in-law, and a weight seemed to leave my shoulders. If Seth could get ahold of Sanford, we could finally get a little justice for what happened to Adam. Maybe I could actually face him again without being completely ashamed of myself.

And if Seth really was about to finish all of this, that meant I could really focus on Indie.

"Good news?" Indie asked quietly.

I nodded, still gripping my phone. "I hope so."

Why did she stop walking?

Catching my confusion, Indie gestured to the building behind her. "This is me," she said awkwardly.

"You *live* here?" I asked before I could stop myself, or at least phrase it better. The building was falling apart, almost literally, and it sat wedged between two equally dilapidated buildings that both looked either empty or ill-used. The entire street looked that way, and I could hardly think anyone would feel safe spending any amount of time there. It made sense why she would walk to the cemetery, though, since it wasn't exactly far away. The coffee shop, however, was way too far, and I could only hope the buses ran through this part of the city.

Indie shrugged. "Not all of us are millionaires," she mumbled, trying to smile. "Thanks for walking me home, even if I didn't need you to."

A couple of twenty-somethings sat on a stairwell across the street in a cloud of smoke, both of their gazes on us. I could hear something or someone rustling through some garbage in a nearby alley, and the nearest street light flickered like we were in some horror movie. "Let me walk you up," I said in a way that told her I wasn't really asking. If I could just get her behind a locked door, I would feel better.

Rolling her eyes, she pulled her keys out of her pocket and led the way through the front door. Inside the building looked even worse, dust coating the floor and the lights dim and the paint either cracking or nonexistent. Thank God the place had no elevator or I might have thought we'd plunge to our death by the time we reached the third floor. The whole place smelled like a combination of urine, cigarette smoke, and worse, and I only kept myself from saying anything about the state of the place because I knew Indie's response would be something along the lines of me being free to leave if it was all so disgusting to me. I felt sick as I followed her up the stairs, and it wasn't because of the smell or the garbage or the dead mouse in the corner.

Indie spent her time stuck in this place, probably because she couldn't afford anything better, and I had an entire house I barely used just because I'd been born to the right parents. I knew the world had never been a fair place, and I had always made sure to never take my circumstances for granted. But this life Indie lived was miserable at best, and she likely thought she didn't deserve any better.

Pausing outside of apartment C3, Indie turned to me with pursed lips. "I know what you're going to say, Matthew," she started, "but—"

"Don't," I said, shoving my hands into my pockets. "You don't have to explain anything. Really." The last thing she needed was a reminder that I had been born to privilege and she to poverty when she had to see it every day surrounding her. It made sense why she would fight so hard for her shop when it was likely the only good thing she had in her life. "I'll see you tomorrow," I told her with a half smile.

Her answering smile was so genuinely sweet that it kept my feet in place for half a second longer than I'd planned to stay, and if I hadn't wanted to catch every moment of it on her lips, I would have missed everything. Indie unlocked her door and pushed it open, and before she even took a step, a hand clapped over her mouth while another pulled her inside by the waist.

I leapt forward and slammed against the door before it could close, and I had my gun in hand as I took in the scene.

Orion had Indie in a powerful hold, and Apollo stood over her with a Glock held expertly in one hand and pointed right at her head. "Welcome, Mr. Davenport," Apollo said as if he hadn't a care in the world.

He knew my name. And he had Indie.

CHAPTER EIGHT

I didn't know who to shoot first. Orion had a knife at Indie's throat; if I went after Apollo, he would kill her in a second. If I tried to shoot Orion (assuming I could even hit him without hurting Indie), Apollo would put a bullet in Indie's head before I could get in another shot. So I stood frozen, my fingers shaking as I frantically searched for a solution.

"You're smarter than you look," Apollo said to me, using the same sing-song voice he'd used before. "Ares was under the impression you would spring right into action."

"Let Indie go," I replied. No matter how hard I tried to keep my gaze on Apollo, I kept looking back at her. She was terrified, ghostly pale and trembling as she tried not to move and injure herself because the knife was pressed so tightly against her neck. She kept her green eyes on me, silently begging me to help.

How do I help her?

Apollo smiled, taking a step closer to Indie so he could touch the point of his gun to her temple. I nearly jumped forward to free her despite the risk of both of us getting killed if I did. "Here's how this is going to go," he said carefully. "I am going to put away my gun. Orion is going to put away his knife. And you are going to step out into the hallway until we've finished talking."

I didn't move. "You've got to be kidding," I said. If he thought there was any chance in hell I was going to—

"Matthew," Indie said.

I stared at her. "Indie, I won't—"

"I'll be fine." Said the girl with a knife at her throat and a gun to her head.

"There, you see?" Apollo grinned, not an ounce of warmth in the expression. "We only want to have a little chat with Fierro. We're not the killing sort." And then he turned his gun on me to meet mine. "Unless we're provoked," he added.

"Matthew, please," Indie begged. How could she ask me to just step outside and let them threaten her like this? It went against everything I was. But with the way she was looking at me, with fear and reassurance and pain and trust and so many things, I found myself slowly walking backward to the door. I wanted so badly to believe she would be okay, because there was nothing I could do about it if she wasn't. If I stepped through that door, she was on her own, and it was killing me doing what she asked.

I didn't think I would survive another Adam situation, especially if I willingly let it happen.

"Two minutes," I told Apollo, and the door clicked shut right in front of me.

A hundred and twenty seconds had never gone by so slowly. I counted them as I paced, wearing holes in the threadbare carpet beneath my feet. I listened hard for any sign of a struggle or a gunshot or any cry of pain, but the door cut me off from everything. Was she even alive? Indie said the police couldn't do anything, but Apollo and Orion were *in her apartment*. They'd clearly broken in, and I knew their faces well enough that with enough firepower we could find them and—

The door opened, and I aimed my gun with a steadier hand than before. The anger was helping. The drive to stop these so-called Greek gods before they hurt anyone else kept my hands from shaking.

But Apollo lifted his hands in surrender, Orion right behind him, and I could see Indie standing unharmed by the window. "You don't know what you're getting yourself into, Davenport," Apollo said as he passed. "Think of your family."

The only thing that stopped me from shooting him right then and there was a whimper from inside Indie's apartment.

Reluctantly letting the Greeks disappear into the stairwell, I rushed inside and immediately pulled Indie into my arms right before she broke. She fell against me, her head on my chest as she started sobbing, and I wrapped one arm around her shoulders and stroked her hair with the other hand, wishing I could do more. But I'd failed her already. I let them break her spirit, and there was nothing I could do to fix it.

All I could do was hold her and hope she didn't send me away again. I wasn't sure I had the strength for that.

"I'm sorry," Indie whispered once she'd found her breath again. She wrapped her arms around my waist and held tight, as if she might fall apart if she didn't. "I know you… I know that was hard."

"I'm just glad you're okay," I said, staring at the darkness in the window. What if something had happened to her because I was stupid enough to leave her side? I didn't care if she wouldn't like it; I wasn't going to let her out of my sight. Ever.

"Can you…" She took in a shaky breath. "I need to sit down."

Though I didn't want to, I let go so she could step over to the sunken couch and collapse on one side. I sat on the other, trying to figure out how to tell her that I wasn't going to leave her even for a second until the Greeks were behind bars or six feet under, whichever came first. She looked so exhausted, still horribly pale and shaking. As soon as she was strong enough, I would take her to my house to hide out until… No, that wouldn't work. The Greeks knew who I was, so they could easily find my house and therefore Indie. There was no way I would put Lanna and her family in danger by taking Indie there. Or to Catherine's. Seth had an apartment somewhere in the city… Even if Apollo managed to find us, no one in his right mind would cross a man like that. At least for now, we could hide with Seth until we found a better solution.

"Matthew?"

As soon as Seth was done with Sanford, I'd give him a call and fill him in on the situation. I was wrong to keep it from him, and if anyone could keep Indie safe—obviously I couldn't—it was Seth.

"Matthew, I need to tell you something."

I forced my thoughts away and focused on Indie. "What?"

She took a deep breath. "When Dante got sick," she said, "the insurance company refused to pay for his treatments."

I stared at her, shaking my head. "Indie, you don't have to—"

"You need to understand," she said. "All of it."

I nodded slowly.

"Dante got too sick to run the shop. It was his baby, his dream since he was a kid, and I think not being able to be there after putting his blood and sweat into the place was killing him faster." A tear slipped onto her cheek, and she brushed it away before I could. "The doctors put him into a coma to try to extend his life until I could find a way to pay for the treatment that would save him, and…"

Slowly, I scooted closer to her and reached out for her hand. She took mine gratefully, squeezing it to find some sort of comfort.

"A loan shark named Zeus offered a way," she continued, "and told me I could borrow the money I needed and pay it back over time. I was desperate, and since Dante was unconscious, I…" I held her hand even tighter. "They did the surgery. Gave him the medications. But he never woke up. The last time I talked to him was before they induced the coma, and I told him I was going to watch *Game of Thrones* without him because I didn't want to wait. I was supposed to have more time with him. I didn't get to say goodbye because suddenly he was just gone. And the next month Ares showed up at the shop to collect my payment, and they've been coming ever since, and I don't have any money left and I don't know what to do. I don't know what to do, Matthew."

I felt like I was being torn in half. Whoever this Zeus person was, I wanted to find him and beat him to a pulp for taking advantage of a young woman whose husband was literally on his deathbed. At the same time, I wanted to wrap my arms around Indie and never let go. She'd been through so much. Losing her husband and being tormented by loan sharks and trying to run a business that wasn't even hers—it was amazing she'd lasted so long on her own. I didn't think I knew anyone who was stronger than this girl who had likely fought her last fight, and for once I knew exactly how to help her.

"I'll pay it," I said easily. I couldn't have said it before, but now there seemed to be a stronger bond between us. She had opened up about her troubles, and I had the perfect solution.

Blinking away her tears, Indie stared at me. "What?"

"Your debt. I'll pay it. No matter how much."

But she shook her head. "I can't let you do that," she said.

"Why not?" I asked. "Like you said, we can't all be millionaires, but those of us who are have some cash to spare."

Why wasn't she smiling? Relaxing with relief? Pulling one hand free, she pressed her palm to my cheek and smiled sadly. "If I let you pay my debt," she said, "that only makes me owe you instead of Zeus. It doesn't solve my problem."

I had a feeling I knew exactly how she would argue if I told her it would be a gift and I wouldn't want to see a penny of it back. Why wouldn't she let me help her?

"Besides," she added, "Zeus would know it was you, and you don't want to get in the middle of this. For your family's sake as well as yours."

Bringing up my family's safety was likely the only thing that could have stopped me from arguing. I leaned a little into her touch, keeping my grip firm on her hand. If I couldn't solve her problem with my money or my gun, what good was I? "How do I help you, Indie?" I finally asked.

Leaning forward, she pressed her lips against my forehead and left a spot of heat behind. "You can go home," she said with a smile. "Get some rest. This is my consequence to deal with, not yours."

Make it mine. Please. How could I possibly leave her behind? "Let me stay the night," I begged. "Bunk on the couch in case they decide to come back."

She was probably too tired to argue or she would have physically removed me from the apartment. Instead, she just looked down at the couch beneath us and frowned. "It's not very comfortable," she said softly. "Dante always said it had character, but it's really just a broken frame."

I'd slept on worse and wouldn't mind at all, but I desperately wanted her to smile. I needed something to get the image of her with a gun at her head out of my mind, and her tears weren't exactly doing the trick. "Are you suggesting I share the bed?" I asked, raising an eyebrow.

"Idiot," she replied and lightly punched me in the arm. But she smiled, if only a little, and I was already starting to feel a little bit better. If I could get her to laugh…

"You keep calling me that," I said with a slight frown, "but I'm starting to think you don't know what it means."

She tried to hit me again, but I caught her hand and easily interweaved our fingers. "Is this supposed to protect me from Ares?" she asked, nodding to our clasped hands. There was a playfulness in her question that threatened to break through my mock seriousness.

"Well yes," I said. "Everyone knows he's a romantic at heart and could never attack someone in…" I swallowed the word that nearly slipped out. That would have made things…complicated. Confusing.

Indie cocked her head, one eyebrow dipping a little lower than the other as she studied me. "You know," she said, "you are nothing like I expected."

I swallowed again. If she kept looking at me like that, I might have tried smoothing the lines from her forehead and ended up getting a little too close. My heart was already beating weirdly as it was. "You didn't know who I was when you met me," I said, "so that probably threw things off."

"That's not what I meant," she replied, shaking her head and gazing at me a little too deeply. "Everything about you is just so…"

"Moronic?" I supplied.

She snickered a little. Not quite a laugh yet, but it was close. "Maybe, but I was going to say contradictory. You come from money but pretend you don't, and you act all tough but you're more sensitive than I think even you realize, and you dress one way but act another."

I grimaced. "You're not bringing up my horrible date last night, are you?" Wait, was it really only last night? It felt like a lifetime ago.

Her smile nearly undid me, pulling me closer. "Even I know not to wear jeans into *Les Madeleines*," she said and dropped her head onto my shoulder.

Hang on. I wasn't equipped for that. *Focus on the conversation, Matthew.* But it was almost impossible when I could smell the lavender of her shampoo so easily. "What were you doing there, anyway?" I asked, working hard to keep my voice steady. "That's where all the rich snobs go to sneer at each other and see who can buy the most expensive steak just so they can throw a picture of it on Instagram then eat just the side salad."

She laughed softly, throwing my heart into a sort of spasm as she settled even heavier against me. What was happening? "Is that really how you see your people?" she asked.

"*My people*? Are we some sort of alien species or something?"

"I was having dinner with my mother-in-law," she replied, and her words slurred a little. She was falling asleep. On my shoulder. *What do I do?* "She remarried into money last year and chose the restaurant. We always go out to eat the night before."

"The night before what?"

"The day Dante died." She snuggled closer, wrapping her left hand around my arm as her fingers tightened around mine. Did she even know she was doing it, or was she half asleep already? Did she have any idea what she was doing to me? "She keeps offering to buy the shop so she can turn it into some sort of health food smoothie place with a little coffee on the side, but Dante built that shop with his own hands. It's all…" She yawned. "It's all I have left of him, and I can't bear to let her change any of it."

"So don't," I said, my whole body tense.

Indie didn't reply, which meant she'd fallen asleep.

And I refused to move an inch, because even though I was completely exhausted, I had no intention of waking her up. Not when I was pretty sure I was falling in love with her. When had that happened?

CHAPTER NINE

I woke suddenly, my head snapping up from the back of the couch and my muscles protesting with sharp shocks of pain with every movement. I couldn't remember falling asleep, and I certainly didn't remember Indie moving from my shoulder to my lap. She actually looked peaceful lying there in the dim dawn light coming in from the window, and I wished I'd stayed asleep so the moment didn't end. Why did I wake up, anyway? I was pretty sure it was ungodly early.

My phone. It was ringing, singing "Killer Queen" much too loudly.

Careful not to wake Indie, I slipped my hand into my pocket and squinted at the screen as the light tried to blind me. "Why?" I groaned under my breath then clicked the answer button. "Catherine, do you have any idea what time it is?"

"Hello, Mr. Davenport."

I sat up straight, rousing Indie but too focused on the unfamiliar voice to worry about that. "Who is this?" I demanded. "Where's Catherine?"

"Oh, she's fine," the woman on the other end replied. "For now."

Indie sat up slowly, turning to me with a question in her eyes.

"Give me proof," I demanded. She had Catherine's phone, but that didn't necessarily mean anything. I didn't have to get worried. Yet.

A message dinged on my phone, and I pulled it away from my ear to stare at the picture. It was definitely Catherine, and she was passed out against a wall, almost like she'd been thrown there. She didn't look good, and my heart sank into my stomach.

"I want to know she's alive," I said, my voice breaking on that last word. I was supposed to look after her. I promised Seth I... What had I done?

The woman laughed, and it sounded just as cold as her voice. "You and I both know Catherine Davenport is worth far more alive than dead."

I could see Indie trying to catch my attention, but I focused my gaze on the opposite wall so I wouldn't miss anything. I couldn't have any distractions. "What do you want? Money? Just tell me how much and it's yours."

"It's not your money I'm after," she replied. What good was a fortune if it couldn't save anyone? "But that's not a discussion for the phone, Mr. Davenport. I'd rather talk things over in person, if you don't mind."

I did mind. Any form of agreeing to her terms would give her that much more power over me, and going to an unknown location would make things much more dangerous for both Catherine and me. But what could I do? This was my baby cousin who was as much a sister as Lanna was. I couldn't just abandon her and hope I was smart enough to find a way to save her. Without knowing where she was, without any idea who I was even talking to, there wasn't much I could do at all except listen and agree to as few of her terms as possible.

"I'm listening," I said. "Tell me where to go."

"Matthew," Indie said, grabbing my hand and keeping it from shaking. In the infinitesimal amount of time before the woman spoke again, I tried to find some sort of strength in Indie's eyes but found only worry and fear to mirror my own.

"You have fifteen minutes to get to the location I just sent to your phone, which I am monitoring to make sure you don't make any calls or take any detours. Come alone, or the girl dies." The line went silent, and the call ended.

Pulling my phone from my ear, I looked down at the text with the address, realizing I didn't have much time to waste if I wanted to get there in time. "I have to go," I said and jumped to my feet.

Indie did too and reached out, grabbing my phone with surprising speed and turning pale when she saw the location. "It's Zeus," she whispered with wide eyes. "She's going after you because of me."

Zeus was a she? It didn't matter. I had to get to Catherine, and I had to move fast. "It's not your fault," I said and hurried to pull my shoes back onto my feet. I had to get to my car, but it was back at the cemetery, which meant I would have to use precious time to run back that way. "She's going after me because I got in her way."

"Matthew, you can't go." She tried to grab my arm, but I slipped out of her grip. "She's going to be a step ahead of you no matter what you do."

Not if I got a step ahead of *her*. "Give me your phone," I said, taking it from her and typing in Seth's number. But the call went straight to voicemail, which meant he was still hunting down Sanford. I cursed and took a shaky breath; I didn't have any other cards to play.

"Matthew," Indie begged, reaching for my hand and holding fast. "Please. It's too dangerous."

I didn't care. "It's Catherine," I told her. What more explanation could I give? "I don't have a choice. And I'm running out of time." I got as far as the door before Indie finally let go of my hand. But as soon as the connection broke between us, I froze, staring at the doorknob and feeling Indie's absence a little too acutely. There was a high chance I could fail and die, and if I didn't make it out, I wanted to…

She was only half a step away, but it felt like I crossed a continent as I took her in my hands and kissed her, memorizing every second of the moment until I knew I was out of time. Without a backward glance, I pulled the door open and rushed out, letting that kiss be the last thing I ever knew of Indiana Fierro.

I felt like I was reliving the past as I pulled into the parking lot, not knowing if I'd been fast enough to save the girl who didn't deserve the pain she'd gone through. The first time Catherine was kidnapped, I'd nearly been too late. As I climbed out of my car and approached the warehouse in front of me, I prayed I was lucky one more time. Even if I didn't make it out, as long as I could get Catherine to safety, everything would be okay.

The door opened before I even reached it, and Ares stood there waiting to greet me, looking way too smug for someone who'd been afraid of me for two weeks. "Boss is inside," he said and held out his arms. I took the hint, doing the same even though my gun was still sitting back on Indie's rickety kitchen table where I'd left it last night. Taking my keys and pocketing them, Ares patted me down until he was sure I had no weapons, and then he jerked his head down the empty hall.

A beefy man I hadn't met greeted me at a corner and gestured for me to turn left. A hundred feet in that direction brought me to Orion, who almost laughed as he placed a hand on my shoulder and led me another fifty feet to a steel door that opened before we even reached it. No matter her flaws, Zeus certainly understood efficiency. The door slid open onto what looked like an old factory floor that was mostly empty aside from a few broken-down conveyors along the far wall and half a dozen support beams. Two desks sat in the middle, pushed together at right angles. A young woman typed away at a computer on the left desk, and an older woman sat behind the one facing me. I had to assume the older was Zeus.

"Thank you, Orion," she said as she elegantly rose to her feet. She sounded even colder than on the phone, her expression matching her tone. There was something…off…about her. She was somewhere in her forties, with stylishly curled brown hair and dark eyes, and the navy pantsuit she wore gave her the appearance of a businesswoman or realtor. But despite all that normalcy, she didn't look human. There was no emotion behind those eyes.

Orion released my shoulder, but a quick glance back told me he hadn't gone far and the other guy was close behind him. They were there to keep me in place, an effective hold without the need for rope or handcuffs. Even if I tried to run, they blocked the only exit I could see.

I took a deep breath. "Where is Catherine?"

Zeus smiled, and it twisted her face without warmth. "Mr. Davenport, I really thought it would be harder to get you here. I'm a little disappointed."

My stomach flipped, my heart picking up its pace again. I didn't like the sound of that. "What do you mean?" I asked.

She waved a hand toward me. "Give your cousin a call. Then maybe you'll understand."

Confused, I pulled out my phone and dialed, lifting it to my ear and turning my eyes back to Zeus. *Don't answer*, I silently begged. *Don't tell me I came here for nothing.*

"Matthew?" Catherine's voice croaked through the speaker. "Is something wrong? What time is it?"

Orion grabbed my phone and ended the call before I could even get a word in.

She wasn't… Catherine was fine. Zeus hadn't even touched her. How did…?

Zeus gestured to the girl behind the computer, and the girl turned the screen to show me an old tabloid article with the exact picture I'd been sent that morning. "It wasn't hard to find something convincing," Zeus said with a roll of her eyes. "And all I had to do was have Athena piggyback from your phone and trick it into thinking it received a call from Catherine's number. Like I said, I'm a little disappointed how easily I got you here. From what my men told me, you were a little more…" Her eyes slid over the length of me. "Formidable."

"So…" I could hardly breathe as my tired brain tried to keep up. "Catherine's not here. You didn't touch her."

"Oh please," Zeus said as she sat back in her chair, "do you really think anyone could lay a finger on that girl and survive now that she's got an actual Olympian for a fiancé? You, on the other hand, won't be missed for a while, and I would imagine your value ripens with time."

It was a trap. For me? "You said you weren't after money," I said. None of this made sense.

"I said I wasn't after *your* money," she corrected as Apollo came into view behind her, his grin a bit overly conceited for someone who wasn't smart enough to work for himself instead of for a frightening woman who probably spent all day in that chair.

Behind me, my phone started to play "Killer Queen" again, probably Catherine trying to make sure I hadn't just pocket-dialed her.

Zeus smiled again, the same twisted grin that made my skin crawl. If not for that dead expression, she would have been a beautiful, normal woman and never in a million years someone I would suspect to run an operation like this. Once the music stopped, she returned to her explanation: "While you have your own fortune, I'm more interested in the combination."

"Combination?" I breathed. How could I have gotten myself into so much trouble in such a short amount of time?

"Davenport," Zeus replied. "Munroe. Hastings. You, my friend, have quite the deck of cards in your hand." She wasn't just after me. She was after my entire family, and I had no way to tell any of them to keep clear and let her do whatever she wanted to me. But I wasn't about to be the reason they lost everything. I got myself into this mess, and I was going to deal with the consequences of that stupidity.

And being just a little more stupid probably wouldn't make things worse. Maybe it would even speed things along. Ever since I sobered up after my spiraling days following Ben's death, I hadn't been particularly fond of things being overly serious, and Zeus sitting all high and mighty in her swivel chair and smiling like she had the winning hand was definitely too serious. Grinning, I figured I should lighten things up a bit.

My laugh echoed through the empty warehouse and wiped Zeus's face clean of her ridiculous smile. I felt Orion and his buddy inch a little closer to me, and Apollo stepped forward with his hand ready to grab his gun. "I'm sorry," I said, keeping my eyes locked on Zeus. "I just… It's funny how little you know about my family."

Her eyebrows pulled together the slightest bit, and she turned to Athena beside her for an explanation. But the girl at the computer shrugged, watching me with curiosity, and no one was quite sure how to react to my comment. "I'm not sure what you mean, Mr. Davenport," Zeus said.

Over the years I'd gotten very good at hiding my real emotions. They often hurt the people around me, and if I kept them secret, I could make sure my loved ones were happy and unburdened. I just hoped I hadn't lost the skill. I needed to lie, and I needed to do it well. It was the only way I was going to make it through this, even if I didn't survive. I desperately needed a laugh. Shrugging, I took a step closer to the woman and felt my guards do the same as Apollo tensed. "Do you really think they'd be willing to rid themselves of their fortunes?" I asked. "For *me?*"

It was Apollo who looked the most shaken, coming up and leaning his hands on Zeus's desk. "Why wouldn't they?" he asked, ignoring the glare his boss gave him.

I folded my arms and carefully kept my smile the same, even though I was definitely excited to break through Apollo's careful control. "I'm the family disappointment," I said. I didn't like how easy it was to say it, though. It might have been a little too true. "My own parents gave up on me years ago, my sister thinks I'm useless, my cousin spends way too much energy trying to marry me off and get me off her hands, and my uncle will tell you all about how I'm ruining the family name with my drunken, lazy ways." That last bit wasn't at all an exaggeration, and Catherine's father would happily tell Zeus all about my wasted potential as a Davenport. I was pretty sure he would ruin us all if he could. "I couldn't even protect my own brother-in-law," I continued, though my voice sounded a little strained and I'd need to rein in the truth if I wanted to throw the Greeks off. "So what makes you think they'll even listen to you?"

Athena typed furiously on her computer, and Zeus leaned in to mutter something to Apollo, and I stood there with a steady grin that wasn't completely faked. They probably wouldn't believe me, but at least I had them questioning themselves.

"Ma'am," Athena said quietly and scooted away so Zeus could see whatever she'd pulled up on her screen.

Apollo looked too, his eyebrows pulling together in concern as he examined the computer. "He's telling the truth," he said just loud enough for me to hear.

I never would have thought I would be glad for the tabloids and chat rooms. With everything flying around about Adam getting shot, there was probably plenty of fodder to feed my lie, which meant I might actually be able to get away from this. Assuming I didn't mess it up like everything else, of course.

Zeus took a deep breath then turned her attention back to me, waving Apollo back to a decent distance. "The world can think what they want of you, Mr. Davenport, but I think you've seriously underestimated your value." *That would be a first.* "I think I'll keep you around for a little while longer, and we'll see if we can't convince that awful family of yours to show a little mercy to their wayward relation. Heracles, find our guest a nice spot to relax until he's rescued, will you?"

The man behind me grabbed my arm in a painful grip and jerked me to the left, pulling me toward one of the broken conveyors. A convenient chain hung on one side of the machine, complete with a set of handcuffs that had likely been used many times before.

"Has Zeus caught many millionaires before?" I asked as Heracles swiftly locked the cuffs around my wrists behind me.

Grunting, Heracles took hold of my shoulder and forced me down to the ground, and I bit back a curse of pain and tried to look as comfortable as possible. If I could just show them I wasn't afraid, maybe they would start to worry. Or maybe they would take it as a sign that I knew my family would pay the ransom. Maybe I'd made a wrong decision.

Wouldn't be the first time.

"Not much of a talker, are you?" I asked while my silent friend double-checked the chains to make sure I couldn't go anywhere. "Are you the one I ask for some coffee or a muffin or something? I didn't exactly have time for breakfast. Maybe you could—"

He cut me off with a strong backfist that knocked me into the machine, doubling the hit to my head and making my ears ring. *Ow.* As my vision blurred a little bit, I shook my head clear and worked my jaw.

"Wow," I said. "No wonder she named you Hercules."

"Heracles," he growled.

I grinned as I asked, "Isn't that what I said?" then grunted as he delivered another powerful blow that stung more than the first, which probably meant he'd cut my cheek or at the very least left a nasty bruise. *Worth it.*

"Heracles," someone else said, and I looked up as Apollo came to join us in our little corner of the warehouse. "Not until after the video."

Ah, what the hell. They were already going to kill me, so I might as well have some fun. "Oh, is there an orientation video?" I asked. "That'd be helpful, because I'm getting all you guys mixed up, and I—" I flinched away from Heracles's fist, this time managing to avoid him.

Apollo crouched down to be at my level, and he grabbed my face and turned it to look at my injuries. "Well, at least this will gain some sympathy," he said.

Still grinning, I shook my head. "They'll think I deserved it," I countered. "You're playing the wrong game if you think you're going to get anything for me."

"Zeus doesn't think so," Apollo said.

"And you agree with everything she does?" I asked.

He frowned. I was getting to him. "She's been doing this a long time."

"And obviously you haven't. How old are you, anyway? Fifteen? Fou—" His fist in my gut cut my jab short, and I collapsed over myself as much as I could while being chained to the machine behind me. "Ah, that one hurt," I wheezed. He had an impressive arm, I'd give him that. But he also had an ego, and that was something I could work with.

"You'd probably do well to keep your mouth shut," Apollo said. He rose, returning to the desk and taking Heracles with him.

"I'm still waiting on that coffee!" I shouted after him, though I could only get so much air into the words as my gut still recovered. Man, I did not expect a guy like that to be that strong, and I told myself to be more careful and not let myself be surprised again. It was the only way I might survive this.

"Still want decaf?" Indie asked behind me.

I nearly shouted a curse but bit back the word, almost choking on it as I forced myself to keep my head forward so no one else would know I was possibly hearing voices. "Indie?" I whispered.

"Definitely decaf," she replied, and I felt her shift the chain as if examining it for weak points.

"What the hell are you doing here?" I asked and turned my head just enough to try to catch a glimpse of her.

"Stop talking, you idiot, or they'll think you're going crazy and come to investigate. I'm here to rescue you. Obviously."

I didn't think she would be so stupid. It didn't matter how glad I was to know she was here, because if anyone caught her, there'd be hell to pay, and I would have that on my head on top of everything else. "Indie, get out of here."

"Ha!" The chain clinked against the machine, and I tensed, though no one in the warehouse seemed to have heard it. "You forget I'm your boss," Indie said, a little softer than before. "I get to tell you what to do, not the other way around. Now shut up and look pretty while I figure out how to get you out of here."

My face definitely burned red, which wasn't exactly something I could hide. Luckily, Orion and Heracles were laughing as Heracles demonstrated his painful punches, and Apollo was deep in conversation with Zeus and Athena. They all seemed convinced I had nowhere to go, but I wasn't sure how long that would last. Apollo said something about a video, which meant before long he would shove a camera in my face and make me beg for rescue. That would most likely happen sooner than later.

But something seemed to have changed in Indie since I left her apartment. Gone was the terrified girl who had given up on everything. The woman behind me sounded confident. Strong. Perfect.

"You like telling me what to do, don't you?" I asked, trying not to move my mouth.

Indie laughed a little. "Maybe more than I should."

Oh, I definitely liked this girl. Maybe more than I should.

"You wouldn't happen to know how to pick handcuffs, would you?" she asked, and the lightness in her tone nearly made me smile.

These little moments when she wasn't worried about her shop or intimidated by the Greeks, she was absolutely adorable. I hoped this version of Indie stuck around.

"Do you have a bobby pin?" I asked.

I could have sworn I heard her roll her eyes. "Why didn't I think of that?" she muttered, clearly annoyed with herself. "But I've never picked handcuffs before. What am I supposed to do?"

How was I going to teach her to pick handcuffs when I had very little time and no way to demonstrate? I knew she was smart, but picking the lock wasn't exactly easy, even with visual guides. It had taken me almost an hour to do it when I learned, and I had no way of knowing when Apollo might be back to take his video.

Still, now I wasn't only worried about myself. I had to make sure Indie got out too. I had to try. "Open it up to a ninety-degree angle," I told her quickly. "Then tear the little rubber piece off the end of the straight side."

"Done."

"Now it gets hard," I continued, taking a deep breath. If I couldn't explain it right, we would only be wasting time and putting Indie at risk of being caught. "Do you see the lock?"

"This little hole right here?" she asked, and her fingers brushed mine.

It took all my strength not to grab her hand just to know she was really there. "Stick the end of the bobby pin about halfway into the hole and use the lock to bend the end."

"Like this?" She pressed the pin to my fingers to let me feel.

"Perfect. Now stick it in half of that and bend it the other way. Like an S." Once I determined she'd done it right, I took another breath. How could I possibly explain this part without her knowing how the key functioned? "Okay, you need to push that end into the top of the lock and turn it."

"Which way?"

I had to think about it, feeling the cuff and trying to figure out which way it moved. "Clockwise," I said. "Or maybe… No. Clockwise."

"You sound really convinced there," she said, and her warm breath brushed the back of my neck and sent a chill through me.

"Try it both ways then," I replied, still fighting a smile. I absolutely hated she was here and putting herself in danger, but that didn't mean

I wasn't glad to feel her behind me.

Indie fiddled with the cuffs for several seconds, her movements growing more frantic as she tried to free me. "It's not working," she said, finally sounding a bit worried. "It has been way too long since I picked a lock."

I chose to ignore that last part for now, as much as I badly wanted to know everything about her past. Knowing she probably wouldn't leave me behind to save herself, I grabbed her fingers and held them tight. "You can do this," I told her gently. "I know you can." She had to, or I would have no way to save her, and I couldn't fathom the guilt I would feel if something happened to her because of my stupidity.

"You don't know me at all," she argued, though she clasped my hand between both of hers.

"And I'd like to fix that," I said, "but I can't do it if I'm chained to a machine."

Apollo and Zeus were getting into an argument while Athena tried to slink away and stay out of it. Heracles and Orion were both thoroughly entertained by the power struggle and had their backs to us. If ever there was a time for us to run, it was now.

"You can do this, Indie. I trust you."

Indie pulled her hands away, and a few seconds later she had one side of the cuffs open. I immediately turned enough to grab the pin from her hand and quickly unlock the other side without looking at her. If I looked at her, I wasn't sure I would be able to look away.

"Is there another way out of here?" I asked. There was no way she'd just waltzed in through the same door as me without someone noticing.

Grabbing my hand, Indie pulled me behind the machine and helped me up to my feet. "There's an emergency exit this way," she said.

"But won't that set off the—"

"Alarm's been dead for years." She led me around another machine, ducking beneath an exhaust vent that jutted straight into the wall.

While I was glad we had a way out, she spoke about it a little too easily. "How do you know this?" I asked with some trepidation. We paused behind another machine, and Indie kept her focus on the door I could see just ahead as I glanced around to make sure we couldn't be seen by anyone.

"I... I've been here before," she said quietly. "A few times. When I was a kid."

My heart beat a little faster. Her reluctance to explain and the timeline in relation to her husband's death could mean only one thing: Indiana Fierro was a little more involved in Zeus's operation than I wanted to think about.

"We need to go," she said and pulled me toward the door.

But Ares stepped into our path, his smile wide. My heart skittered into overdrive, and I moved in between him and Indie, but I quickly realized my efforts to protect her were pointless. Ares's eyes immediately dropped to our clasped hands. Folding his arms, he shook his head and muttered, "I should have known," just as Orion and Heracles came up behind us, cutting off any chance of retreat. "Zeus will want to talk, Fierro," he said to Indie and jerked his head for us to follow.

I thought about trying to fight my way out, but this was not the time to be reckless.

This was the time to accept that things weren't looking good. And the fact that Indie didn't seem at all nervous as she guided me along behind Ares was just as disconcerting. If she wasn't actually afraid of these people, what did that mean for me? Or for *us*? I kept hold of her hand even as my mind spun; if I let go, I wasn't sure I would get the chance to hold her again.

Zeus hadn't left her chair, but she stood when she caught sight of us. Apollo behind her kept his glare on Indie. "Ares," Zeus said with a nod.

Grabbing my arms and forcing them painfully behind me—and out of Indie's grip—Ares kicked my legs and knocked me to my knees. "Easy," I grunted, all too aware that Indie remained untouched and on her feet. At least they weren't hurting her, but that only sort of made me feel better.

Stepping around the desk, Zeus approached us and twisted her mouth into that grotesque smile of hers. "Artemis," she said, sounding every bit the happy mother to see a lost child. She even held out her arms as if to wrap Indie in a loving hug. "It's been too long."

So Indie had her own Greek name? *Awesome.*

Indie blinked a tear onto her cheek and shook her head. "That's not my name," she said, her voice steady but threatening to break.

"It was once," Zeus replied and shifted her smile into a frown. "I thought we were friends."

"I thought you were above violence," Indie said.

Zeus's eyes slid over to my bleeding face, which was already getting stiff. "Heracles was having a little fun," she said with a shrug.

"I'm not a personal punching bag," I growled back but immediately regretted it when Ares twisted my arms and sent sharp pain through my shoulders.

"Be nice, Ares," Zeus scolded, though she looked a little too pleased by my groan of pain. "So, Artemis, you decided to come back after all. You have no idea how happy that makes me. But for that?" She pointed at me, and I scowled.

Indie barely gave me a glance. "I came back because he doesn't deserve this from someone like you. He was only trying to help me, and—"

"And he got in my way," Zeus replied, shaking her head. "You know I don't like when people mess with things they shouldn't. I never planned to hurt him."

"Threatening his family *does* hurt him," Indie argued, and I looked up at her in surprise. "They're the only thing he cares about." How did she know that? I hadn't told her anything about my family, and according to the internet, I was a disgrace to my family name. "Even if you do get a ransom," she continued, "what good is it going to do you when he can just turn around and take you down the second you let him go?"

I swallowed as Zeus narrowed her eyes. That probably wasn't the best thing to say, and Indie trying to help would likely make things worse. Now Zeus had more leverage on me, knowing she only had to threaten my family to get me to cooperate completely. The moment she made a legitimate threat on any of them was the moment I would give in without question.

"You make a good point, Artemis," Zeus said slowly, turning and giving Apollo a look that made him go a little pale. He was probably the mastermind behind this idea to lure me here, and his plan was starting to fall apart. "We may need to reconsider for a moment. Orion, be a dear and help Ares secure both of them. Properly, this time."

Ares lifted me up by my arms, using so much force that I actually cried out from the pain. Chuckling, he forced me toward one of the steel support beams and shoved me down to its base.

"You'll pay for that," I growled, though I really didn't have much to threaten him with. He'd already beaten me once, and the last several minutes had sorta killed the fight in me. My family was still in trouble. Indie was a Greek. Now it wasn't just my life on the line but probably hers as well. And no matter how I might have felt about her (I was beginning to doubt), it didn't change the fact that I really knew nothing about her. She'd said it herself.

Ares used a zip tie to secure my arms around the beam behind me while Orion did the same to Indie on the opposite side, and then they left to rejoin their boss in a huddle to decide what to do with us.

Dropping my head against the beam, I closed my eyes and took a deep breath. No matter what happened, I had to make sure my family stayed safe, and I could at least get Indie out of the warehouse. I didn't care what happened to me as long as they all remained well and whole. But first I needed a plan.

"I'm sorry, Matthew," Indie said suddenly. "This is all my fault."

I couldn't exactly blame her for everything, but my poor-to-begin-with plans were quickly unraveling. "I don't want to talk," I said. I needed to focus. How could I free Indie and distract the Greeks long enough for her to run? Heracles had vanished, and without knowing where he was, I couldn't be sure which path she should take to get out.

"Matthew, please."

Zip ties were difficult but not impossible to get free of. The beam behind us was the biggest obstacle.

"At least let me explain."

Oh, Indie was still talking. And it sounded like she was crying. I paused my planning and turned my head enough to see her out of the corner of my eye. "What?" I asked, though maybe I shouldn't have sounded so impatient because something close to a sob broke out of her. *Oops.*

"Look," she said, "I met Dante when I was nineteen because I was trying to steal his wallet. Zeus was more like the Fagin to my Oliver Twist back then, and she took me in and gave me a place to stay when I needed one most. And she wasn't like this back then."

That made sense, and though I had a million questions about her childhood and why she even needed Zeus in the first place, I had more pressing things to think about, like the fact that Apollo glanced our way every few seconds and wasn't planning to let us out of his sight again.

"I was only with her for a couple of years," she continued, "and Dante was the one who got me out. He gave me a job, a home, a *future*, and I stopped being Artemis and went back to being Indie. We got married, and I traded Jones for Fierro, and together we turned the shop into something good. Until he got sick, I didn't contact Zeus even once. You have to believe I wasn't any part of this."

Of course I believed that. I hadn't even doubted her in the first place. Not really. But… "Your last name was Jones?" I asked. "Seriously?" Like the professor indeed…

"Oh my God," she groaned. "That's what you care about?"

I almost laughed, though the cluster of goons nearby made that a little hard to do. "I just think it's funny that—"

"I'm trying to apologize, idiot. It's my fault you're in this mess, and I shouldn't have even let you get involved in the first place. But the shop was struggling, and I didn't have the money to pay Zeus, and… I failed him, Matthew. I promised Dante I would look after the shop, and I can't do it. I can't even look after myself, and I'm going to lose it all."

I hated hearing that pain in her voice. Worse, I hated knowing there was nothing I could do to comfort her, not when I was tied to the other side of a beam. But maybe there was something I could say, some way to help her know she couldn't give up just because she met a road block. But doing that would require me to talk about myself, and there were some things I didn't talk about with anyone. Not since Luke.

Indie would have to be the exception.

"Did you know I was homeless for almost a year?" I said, breaking the silence.

Indie sniffed. "What? But you're—"

"Matthew Davenport, I know. I was twenty-six at the time, had just finished a tour, and my parents wanted nothing to do with me. They cut me off before I even graduated high school, when I first enlisted, and I hadn't seen a penny from them in years." I sighed, wishing I didn't have those dark years to haunt me. But they were important, and I had to keep talking.

"My older brother died when I was seventeen," I said, "and I took it hard. Too hard. I turned to drinking and nearly got kicked out of the military more than once because I could barely keep myself together. And after that tour, I just couldn't handle it anymore. All of my money went to the bars, and I was evicted from my apartment. I had no friends, no family who would take me, and I spent nine months sleeping in parks and alleyways and shelters. At one point my demons got so bad that I nearly…" I swallowed. If Luke Hawthorne hadn't found me behind the bar that night and talked me out of it, I wouldn't have been around to even talk about this. He had become my best friend for a reason.

"It doesn't matter," I continued. "All I'm saying is I know what it feels like to lose everything. To feel like you've failed everyone you love and there's no way you could ever come back from that. But it's not true. Someone will come along and help you through it, and looking back, you'll realize that without those losses you wouldn't be who you are. And you wouldn't be this strong or this brave."

I couldn't move much, but I reached as far as I could and touched her arm.

She did the same to me, and it felt like something had changed between us in the last couple of minutes. What that was, I didn't know, but I hoped we would both be around long enough to find out.

"We're going to get out of this, Matthew," she said quietly, though her voice shook. "I'm still not sure how, but we will."

"You're weirdly optimistic sometimes," I muttered.

"Years of practice," she replied. I understood that well.

Looking over at the Greeks, I tried to figure out our best play. Eventually they would have to cut us free to do whatever they were planning, and I would have a short moment to fight or run or do something drastic enough to give Indie the time to get away. Zeus hadn't shown any particular preference for any of her men, so I couldn't use someone as leverage. Except maybe…

"Indie, do you trust me?"

"What?"

"Do you trust me?"

She hesitated before giving me her answer, but then she said, "Yes," with such conviction that it made my heart start pounding in my chest. The word nearly undid me, but I forced myself to focus.

Orion was coming back, his knife in his hand. Ares was with him. This was our only shot.

"Play along," I said then dropped my hand from her arm just as the Greeks arrived.

"Time to go," Orion said, cutting Indie's tie first then moving to free me.

The second the plastic strip fell from my hands, I moved quickly, grabbing Orion's wrist and twisting hard until he dropped the knife. I snatched the blade, at the same time kicking Orion's knee and forcing him back into Ares, and then I rolled. I grabbed Indie and pulled her into the roll with me until I could sit up with her tight against my chest. I had the knife at her throat before Ares even realized what was happening.

"Stay back," I warned, praying I wasn't wrong.

Orion and Ares were confused but luckily didn't move. Apollo and Zeus came over a moment later, and while Apollo was amused, Zeus looked livid. "What are you doing, Davenport?" she asked, her eyes locked on the knife. I was more partial to guns, but that didn't mean I didn't know how to hold a knife. She could obviously tell I was well-trained. "You're not as good at bluffing as you think you are. You won't hurt her."

"Won't I?" I asked. This *had* to work. Indie's life depended on it. "Didn't you hear what the girl said? My family is everything to me, and I won't let anything threaten them. *Anything.* Even if that means hurting her."

Indie was shaking beneath me. I was playing my part too well, and she was terrified. But there was no way to tell her I would rather die than let her get hurt. I just hoped her trust in me didn't run out before I could show her that.

Zeus put her hand on Orion's shoulder, her other in a fist at her side. I might have imagined it, but her fingers shook a little. She was worried. "Artemis hasn't worked for me in years," she said, and her voice at least was calm. She could bluff too. "What makes you think I care what happens to her?"

Please forgive me for this. I slid the knife just enough to draw blood and get a whimper of pain out of Indie.

Zeus took a step forward, her eyes wide. "What do you want?" she asked. "You want to leave? Fine. Just hand the girl over, and you can go."

"Tempting," I said. But there was no way I was leaving Indie anywhere near these people. "But I'm afraid I don't trust you, so I'll need the girl for insurance. Get up," I told Indie, lifting her to her feet as I stood. She shook even harder, tears streaming down her cheeks, tears I wanted so badly to wipe away. There was no way she was going to trust me after this, but at least she would be alive. That was what mattered, even if it meant I never saw her again.

Holding up one hand, Zeus took another step closer. "You don't have to do this," she said gently. "I'm a woman of my word, and if I say you are free to go, then you're free to go."

"You might be right," I replied, slowly moving toward the door with Indie in tow. "Maybe you won't do anything, but there's no way I believe *he* likes the idea." I nodded toward Apollo, whose glare hadn't left me for a second, and everyone turned to look at him.

Apollo didn't move his gaze even a little. "He is worth so much more than Fierro," he growled. "I am not about to let him walk out of here just because you have a soft spot for the little—"

"You see?" I said loudly, still making my way for the door. "That's why I can't trust anything you say. It sounds like the Sun God isn't so fond of his sister." We were so close. If I could just keep their attention on the power struggle, maybe we could—

"Stop!" Apollo yelled and pulled out his gun.

The logical thing to do would be to keep using Indie as a shield to hold my bluff. But a man was pointing a gun at Indie's chest, and my heart overtook my head and twisted me around so she was safely hidden behind me and I had nothing but a knife to protect me from a bullet.

"I knew it," Apollo said, and those three words sprung everybody into action.

Ares was closest, and he lunged toward me with raised fists. I dodged and turned to kick him down, but Indie beat me to it. She had her knee in his groin and threw her elbow into the back of his neck before I could even get my foot up. "Duck!" she shouted. I slipped beneath Orion's attack and threw my shoulder into his gut, shoving him into the nearest support beam and cracking his head against it. He crumpled beneath me. Ares was on his feet again, though stumbling, and going after Indie, so I leapt forward.

The gunshot brought me to an abrupt halt, stealing my breath.

"No!" Zeus shouted.

But Indie collapsed anyway, a horrific stripe of red painting her side.

Gasping, reeling, I turned to Apollo at the same time as Zeus, and he seemed to realize his mistake when he saw that he was outnumbered. He shook as he shifted his gun between the two of us, trying to decide who was the bigger enemy.

Something slammed into me from behind, knocking me hard into the cement. Ares landed on top of me at the same time Apollo shot again, though his bullet didn't hit Zeus as she ducked behind her desk. I fought Ares off and threw my elbow into his nose, hearing the crack just a second before the blood started pouring. Apollo shot again, the bullet ricocheting off the metal desk, and Ares kicked me hard in the back.

"You imbecile!" Apollo shouted at Zeus. "You threw away a fortune!"

I rolled to get some distance and suddenly found myself directly in the line of his gun. "Oh sh—"

Ares tackled me again, and a bullet disappeared into his torso as he fell on top of me again, this time without moving. I shoved him away as a dark blur—Zeus—sped past my sight, and then I moved as fast as I could, pushing myself up to my feet and charging Apollo before he could kill anyone else. Both of us crashed to the ground, and I landed hard on my back, the impact knocking the air out of my lungs. Apollo scrambled for his gun that had clattered several feet away. I grabbed his foot, pulling him back to the ground.

Crawling forward, I kept Apollo on the ground then dove for the gun before he could reach it. He fought me for it, but I grabbed the barrel and threw the gun as far as I could. Apollo snarled and wrapped his fingers around my neck, but I kicked my knee into his stomach and followed his collapse with a punch to his temple. He tried for a moment to get back up, but then his eyes rolled into the back of his head and he slipped to the floor unconscious.

Finally.

I struggled to my feet, nearly joining him on the ground again as my vision swayed, and then I stumbled over to Indie. "Please don't be dead," I gasped as I fell to my knees next to her and brushed her hair out of her face. "Indie? Indie, talk to me!" I couldn't breathe, and if she was gone, I wasn't sure if I...

She opened one eye, then the other, and lifted her head to make sure everyone else was down. "Sorry," she said, holding her hand to her bloody ribs and slowly sitting up. "He only grazed me, but I figured playing dead was my best option. Maybe I shouldn't have—"

I fell into her, wrapping my arms around her so tight that it squeezed the air from her lungs. But I didn't care. She was alive. Everything was okay. "I'm so sorry," I whispered into her shoulder. "I didn't want to hurt you. I'm sorry."

She brushed one hand through my hair and held me tight as I tried to breathe again. "I wasn't worried about me," she said. "I knew you would take care of me. I'm just glad it's over."

She pulled away from the hug, as I knew she eventually would, and

I let myself fall spread eagle to the ground in exhaustion. "I'm getting too old for this," I mumbled, taking a necessary moment to catch my breath before my heart exploded out of my chest because it was beating so fast. "But it's not over yet." Catching sight of a phone lying near enough to reach, I picked it up and quickly dialed.

"Who are you calling?" Indie asked. "The police?"

"Better," I replied as the call connected. *Thank God he answered this time.* "Hey, Seth. It's Matthew. Listen, I need a favor…"

CHAPTER TEN

The first thing Seth did when he stepped into the warehouse twenty minutes later was burst into laughter. I was too tired to get mad at him, so I just let him get it out of his system as I sat against the wall with Indie in my arms. She, I noticed with pleasure, barely looked at Seth and kept gently touching the cut on my cheek as she tried to decide if I would need stitches or not.

"This is about the last thing I expected to see when I got back this morning," Seth said, his grin wide as he stepped around two annoyed thugs who were gagged and zip-tied together. Ares hadn't been lucky enough to wake up, and we'd left him over by the desk. I assumed Heracles left with Zeus and Athena. "You took out all of them?"

I narrowed my eyes. "Don't sound so surprised. It's not like I'm—ow!"

Indie winced. "Sorry."

Grabbing her hand, I touched her palm to my lips and shook my head. "Don't be sorry," I told her. "Now are you going to let me look at that or not?"

She glanced down at her bloody shirt and shrugged. "I told you I'm fine," she said. "It'll be a nice scar someday."

Wow, I wanted to kiss her. Everything I was feeling for this girl was so foreign that I really couldn't have said what it meant, but I knew without a doubt I would be perfectly content to keep her at my side like she was for a very long time. Maybe even forever. And while I had no idea how she felt about me at this point, I figured I had made some headway in the "get Indie to like me" department. That was something, at least, and I was eager to pursue the idea that she didn't altogether hate me like she used to.

But I had more important things to deal with, mainly the two morons who kept looking at Seth like he was the devil himself come to drag them down to Hell. Groaning as my stiff body protested moving again, I got to my feet and stood next to Seth. "So what do we do with them?" I asked. "Turn them over to the police?"

Seth used his foot to keep Apollo from squirming. "Eventually," he said with a wicked grin. "So which one is the mastermind boss?"

The one who got away.

"Talia Honduras," Indie answered for me, coming to my side and slipping her hand into mine. That was a good sign, and I had a hard time not staring at her in admiration as she continued. "She and Jesse Hunt probably went to their second location on the other side of town until they can get to the storage locker where all their fake identities are waiting. And Athena—Sabrina Masters—likes to think she's a ghost, but her internet trail is pretty easy to follow if you know where to look."

Seth lifted his eyebrows. "I'm impressed," he said. "I'm guessing you know where to look. You wouldn't happen to know where the locker is, would you?"

Indie shrugged, her other hand on her ribs as she looked down at Apollo and Orion. "I don't know, but I'm sure one of them does. And you look like someone who can get that information pretty easily."

Laughing, Seth put his hand on my shoulder—thank God he was gentle—and said, "Looks like I have some work to do. Why don't you take your charming little friend home, and I'll take care of these clowns?"

"Gladly," I said. I had certainly had enough excitement for one day, and I needed to try to convince Indie to go to the hospital to make sure she wasn't injured more than she said she was. But instead of heading for the door, I glanced back at Ares. I wasn't sad that he was gone, but the only reason I was alive was because he wasn't. I almost wished I could thank him, which was a confusing feeling. Plus... "Ares has my car keys," I muttered, frowning. I didn't particularly want to dig through a dead man's pockets.

"Take mine," Seth replied immediately and held out his keychain without taking his eyes off of Apollo. What would I ever do without Seth?

"Thank you," I said, making sure he knew I meant it. "For everything."

"Hey." Touching my arm, Seth grimaced a little as he looked at me. "I know I should have talked to you before I proposed," he said quietly. Was this really the time? "You may not be her father, but you're the closest thing she has to one. If I had thought for a second you might have objected, I wouldn't have asked her. I swear. But I still should have asked. How can I make it up to you?"

Seth Hastings was practically begging for my good favor? Somehow I'd fallen asleep feeling like I had no place in the world and had woken up to a completely new reality. It was a little hard to wrap my head around how things could have changed while staying completely the same. Seth was every bit the good man I knew he was, and Catherine was lucky to have him. So was I.

"Tell you what," I said. "Don't mention a word of this to anyone, and we'll call it even."

Seth grinned. "Deal," he said then crouched down next to Apollo. "So," he said, dropping his voice into his most intimidating growl. "Where can I find your lady friend?"

"We should go," I said to Indie, holding her hand a little tighter. I didn't want her to see Seth at work, and I certainly wasn't about to make her spend any more time in this warehouse than she needed to.

She smiled, the dimple in her cheek out in full force. "Yeah," she agreed. "You look like crap."

How could I ever have doubted I was hopelessly in love with this girl? Yeah, that was what this pounding in my heart had to be. That, or adrenaline… If it wasn't love, I would have hated to figure out how love could possibly top this. I felt like my chest was seconds away from imploding and leaving me a pathetic mess on the floor. It was wonderful.

"Thanks," I replied, pulling Indie just a little closer as we walked through the empty hallways. "I was going for a more natural, rugged sort of look. It's nice to know it's working."

"You're such an idiot," she said, wrapping her arm around my waist.

"I know I am." I easily put mine around her shoulders, and it felt like I had known this girl for years. I was so glad I stumbled into her shop that day. Even if she thought I was an idiot.

Indie wouldn't let me take her to the hospital, so I took her to my house instead. It was better than her apartment, and at least I had a fully equipped first aid kit in the closet. I was exhausted and sore, and a headache pounded in my skull, but I refused to relax until I was sure she wasn't badly hurt.

"Sit," I told her, pointing to the couch as I fished through the kit for some alcohol and gauze.

"Yes, sir," she replied, nearly laughing the words. "Should I drop and give you twenty, too?"

I rolled my eyes but couldn't keep myself from smiling. Indiana Fierro was bossy and infuriating and spent more time insulting me than having actual conversations, and I was falling more and more in love with her every second. How had that even happened? "We'll start with this," I said, sitting next to her and touching my finger to her neck where I'd cut her. "Have I told you I'm sorry about that yet?"

Her smile was warm, and she gave my hand a squeeze. "Many times. And I don't blame you for it."

She should have. Luckily I hadn't cut very deep, and it was a relatively minor cut that would heal quickly. "Now this," I said next, my hand hovering over her ribcage.

Indie took hold of her shirt and lifted it up enough for me to see the groove left by the bullet. My heart ached at the sight of her blood-soaked skin, and the pain of it spread throughout my entire body until it made my fingers shake. That was my fault. Every drop of blood could have been avoided if I'd just stayed out of things like she'd asked.

"I'm so sorry," I whispered, frozen as I stared at the gash. "If I had just… I didn't want you to get hurt, and I pushed my way into something I shouldn't have, and I'm sorry. This is all my fault. I'm—"

"If you say 'I'm sorry' one more time," Indie snapped suddenly, putting her hands on either side of my face, "I am going to slap you. Hard."

"But—"

"Hey!" She leaned so close that she would have had my full attention even if she wasn't speaking so forcefully. "None of this is your fault. You can't control what other people do, Matthew. I made the choice to come after you, and Apollo made the choice to shoot. I know you want to save everyone, but sometimes you can't. Okay? That doesn't make you a bad person. Even if you only manage to save one person your entire life, even if it's just yourself, you're still worth something. Especially to me."

I stared at her, my heart pounding and my stomach twisting and my head spinning because what she said hit me deep in my gut, setting off a chain reaction inside me that felt like dynamite blowing all of my guilt to shreds. I still blamed myself for things going sour, and I would always carry a bit of that guilt no matter what she told me. But with Indie so close that all I had to do was lean forward a little for our lips to touch, maybe I could bear it. Maybe I'd be fine.

I crossed the distance between us slowly, not like the last time. I was in no rush, and I wanted this moment to be absolutely perfect.

Only she shifted her fingers over my mouth, one eye slightly narrowed as she smiled. "You need to sleep, Matthew Davenport."

I groaned, tucking a piece of dark hair behind her ear. "Why?" I asked. "So you can rob me blind?"

"That, and because you look awful. Did you even sleep last night?"

Just her talking about sleep was pulling my eyelids down, but I forced myself to stay awake. "I had some crazy woman trap me on the couch and snore all night," I said, resting my hands on her shoulders.

Grinning with an especially pretty blush, she brushed away my hair from my forehead and muttered, "You could have moved me."

"No, I couldn't have."

Moving her hands to my chest, she gently pushed me back until my head lay on the armrest of the couch. If she kept running her hand through my hair like that, I was…going to… "Sleep," she whispered, and it was the last thing I heard.

It took me a full twenty seconds after I woke up to figure out why I could barely breathe. Something was wrong, and Zeus had found us, and… Indie was sound asleep on top of me, curled up on my chest with her head just below my chin. And I lay there wondering how she could fit so perfectly. Like she was designed to be there. I wished I could see her face as she slept, but I listened to her steady breathing and decided that came as a close second. I wasn't crazy to think she felt safe with me, was I? She hadn't gone home or even chosen to seek out my barely used bed. She'd stayed with me.

The sudden sounds of a phone made me jump, startling Indie awake too, and I frowned my apology before stretching my arm out to grab

Indie's phone from the coffee table. A quick glance at the number told me it was Seth, and I answered the call quickly. "Seth?" I asked as Indie slowly pulled herself off of me so I could sit up.

"Ha!" he said, a little too loudly. "I owe myself a hundred bucks."

Groaning, I rubbed sleep from my eyes then reached out for Indie's hand without thinking. The fact that she slid her fingers between mine almost immediately did me a world of good. "What?" I asked Seth, giving Indie a smile.

The smile she sent back, her eyes brilliantly green in the sunlight streaming in through the window, nearly made me hang up and pull her into a kiss before she could stop me this time.

Seth laughed. "I bet myself this missed call from this morning was the girl's number and that you hadn't left her side. I have your phone, by the way. One of those punks had it in his pocket."

"Did you…" I swallowed as Indie ran her fingers along my arm, being way too distracting. "Were you successful?"

"Your friends Apollo and Orion were both happy to turn themselves in," Seth replied casually, as if discussing the weather. "That Zeus lady puts up a good fight, but as soon as she tried to use her pal Herc as a bargaining chip, he was happy to change sides and hand her over. They're both in custody, and they likely won't get out any time soon after the things Hercules told me."

"Heracles," I mumbled, shivering as Indie touched her lips to my shoulder. Was she *trying* to distract me? Actually, yes. She was. Her grin said so, and I couldn't help but lean closer to her in the hopes of coaxing an actual kiss out of her.

"Yeah, he told me that too," Seth said with a chuckle. Why was he still on the other end? *Hang up.* "Listen, I have some bad news, though."

I sat up straight. "Bad news," I repeated, and Indie went pale.

"I had one of my guys look into the business Zeus was doing, and he said it's all perfectly legal."

I didn't like the sound of that. "Meaning…?"

"Meaning your friend Fierro isn't out of her debt just because Talia Honduras is behind bars. The loan's in her accountant's name instead of hers, so she can still call in the loan when she's behind bars. Zeus may be in jail for what she did to you this morning, but the accountant is free and clear to keep running the business for her. I plan to have a talk with this accountant to make sure he doesn't carry on the legacy of terror, but I don't think there's anything I can do for Fierro. I'm sorry, Matt."

Well that certainly ruined the mood, and I looked at Indie and tried to figure out how best to break the news to her. She had actually seemed happy for a split second, and I didn't want to be the one to destroy that. But even as I looked at her, she seemed to already know as she retreated to the far side of the couch with a pillow held tight in her arms and her gaze on the floor.

"Thanks, Seth," I said quietly. "I owe you one."

"Anything for family, right?"

"Right. Oh, what happened with Sanford?" I asked, though at the moment I didn't particularly care. Not when tears had sprung up in Indie's eyes as her reality sank back in.

Seth waited to answer, and I held my breath. "Sanford's not going to hurt anyone else," he said softly.

I didn't need him to explain. "Go see your fiancée," I replied. "Thanks, Seth. For everything."

Setting the phone back on the table, I slowly moved closer to Indie but didn't reach out for her. I wasn't sure she would want me to. "Indie?"

"I'm going to lose the shop," she replied, blinking a tear onto her cheek. "After everything, I can't believe I'm going to lose it."

What could I say? Practically nothing. "I told you I can pay back the loan. Zeus won't be able to do anything now that she—"

Indie grabbed my hand, shaking her head. "You know why I can't. I'm beyond grateful that you're willing, but..."

I sighed. "But a debt is still a debt. I get it. Even if I let you pay me back over time? I promise I will be a benevolent lender."

"Matthew..."

Yeah, I knew she wouldn't go for it, but it was worth a shot. She had given up. Faced the facts and decided she had done all she could. And though her not wanting my help was hard to swallow, I understood. After everything she'd been through, she didn't want to be a charity case. She wanted to go down on her own terms, and there was nothing I could do but stay by her side and offer what strength I could. Hesitantly, I held my arms out.

Indie immediately crawled into my embrace, and I just held her as she cried. In this moment, at least, I could be helpful, though it was killing me not being able to do more. There had to be a way I could help her. Some way to save that part of her husband so she wouldn't have to lose him completely. I would do anything to make this girl happy. Anything.

CHAPTER ELEVEN

I didn't see Indie for two days. She said it was not because she didn't want to see me but because she was busy with the coffee shop, but when I stopped by the shop to see if I could help, the doors were locked and the lights were off. I walked past her apartment building a dozen times but could never bring myself to walk up the stairs to her door, and I told myself it was so she could have some privacy and peace after her ordeal, not because I was afraid she didn't want me to.

But I was deathly afraid she didn't want me to.

How much time did someone need to recover?

I was alone in a way I'd never felt alone before, and it sucked. Adam called and asked how the new job was going—I told him things were great. He didn't believe me, but at least we were talking again. Lanna texted me multiple times a day as if she sensed something was wrong— I mostly ignored her and hated myself for it. Catherine showed up at my house with an apology dinner after putting me through such a terrible date—I pretended I wasn't home. Even Seth checked in, though he was smart enough to keep the conversation to just a couple of texts. My family was worried, but I didn't have the heart to help them, and for the first time in my life I just wished they would keep to themselves. They couldn't fix this any more than I could, and they would just get that pitying look in their eyes that made my stomach twist itself into knots.

No, they didn't need to make themselves a part of this. I had to handle this on my own.

"What am I supposed to do, Ben?" I asked as I paced in front of his grave two days after our encounter with Zeus. "She won't answer my calls, barely answers my texts, and it's killing me not seeing her. What if she needs me? What if she's hurt, or Zeus got free, or there's someone else out there trying to take advantage of her? What do I do?" I needed to know how to help her.

Luke would have known how to help her. My friend had been good at that, finding the best ways to help people work through their problems, and it was one of the reasons I had become his friend so easily after years of isolating myself. He had gotten Lanna to make her own choices and forge her own path. He had broken Adam out of his shell and taught him how to talk to people. He had convinced me life was still worth living even when things went wrong. He would have known exactly how to make Indie's life easier because he was good like that. Like Ben had been.

But how did I be like them?

The headstone was silent as always, but I wasn't about to accept that response.

"You told me I could come to you with anything," I growled. "That you would always be there no matter where you went. So where are you, Ben? Where's your wisdom when I need it the most?"

Nothing. Seventeen years of coming to this cemetery, and he'd given me a whole heap of nothing.

"Benjamin Harris Davenport, you are a terrible brother if you think I'm going to just stand here and let you treat me like this." I kicked at a clump of grass as I passed. "You'd probably have no problem just waiting patiently for her to let you into her life because you were always the perfect one. 'Why can't you be more like Ben? Why can't you get good grades and be nice to the younger kids and stop getting into fights that don't matter?' Well you know what? I *never* got into a fight that didn't matter. Not once. If I wasn't defending Lanna, I was defending you, and you just looked at me every time I came home with a busted lip or a black eye like I'd disappointed you somehow because I couldn't keep my head down and let people walk all over me."

I paused, looking down at his headstone. "All I wanted," I said, quieter now, "was for you to look at me just once and think 'he'll be okay.' I wanted you to realize that you were the only person whose opinion mattered. You were the only person I looked at and wanted to be. You were everything. And now I need you to tell me how to be the man she needs me to be because if I can't be in her life, I don't... I don't know what the point is anymore. Why did I go through all of that if she's just going to forget me and move on?"

"I didn't forget you."

I turned quickly, my heart jumping into overdrive as Indie stepped up next to me and looked down at Ben's headstone with red eyes. She'd been crying, and I hated that I wasn't there to hold her. "Indie," I muttered.

"I came here to get some advice from Dante," she said without looking at me. "But some idiot was up here shouting at a grave, and it was a little bit distracting." With a small half smile, she lifted her eyes up to me.

I didn't even feel the embarrassment I should have. She was here, and nothing else mattered. "How much did you hear?" I asked.

"Enough. I'm selling the shop."

"What?"

Sighing, she stepped forward and touched the corner of Ben's headstone as if he might talk to her, even though he'd never said a word to me. "It's the only thing I can do now," she said quietly. "And it'll be okay. I can start over."

That shop was everything to her. "But Dante—"

"My husband is gone, Matthew," she said, looking back at me with fresh tears. "I think I was clinging to the hope that somehow he might come back, that if I kept the shop exactly how it was, he would…" Shaking her head, she came back over to me and said, "I don't need a building to help me remember him. But I do need you."

I furrowed my eyebrows. "To help you remember?" That was exactly what I wanted to hear… If I had to compete with her memory of her husband, a man who had changed her life for the better, I wasn't sure there could be a future between us. And that would kill me.

"No, idiot," she replied and slowly wound her fingers through mine. "To help me say goodbye. When I find a buyer for the shop, will you be there with me? I don't know if I'll be able to let go on my own."

It hurt that she even had to ask. "Of course," I whispered. As long as she needed me, I would be there.

Indie was undeniably a wreck. I was worse. She'd spent the last two days cataloguing everything in the shop so she could get the most value, and I had spent the last two days doing everything I could to not fall apart as I helped her. I knew she needed me around, but being so close to her without actually *being* with her was, quite frankly, torture.

When I met Indiana Fierro, I never would have guessed she could have so much power over me. But every second I spent with her, I learned more and more about her past and who she was, and every second, I fell a little more in love with her.

Her parents were high school sweethearts who had Indie young, and they were a poor but blissfully happy family until Indie was sixteen and they died in a car crash, leaving her by herself. Uninterested in going into foster care, she set off on her own under the radar until she met Zeus and was taken under her wing. Eventually she met Dante, who gave her a job at the shop, and they fell in love. Indie was nineteen when she got married. She was only twenty-three when Dante died. For the last two years, she'd been on her own again, only occasionally spending time with her mother-in-law who had never fully approved of the girl from the streets.

I'd known from the start that Indie was fiercely independent, but the more I came to know her, the more I realized how lucky I was she let me stay around at all. She knew who she was and what she wanted, and I just had to hope there was a chance she wanted me.

By the morning of the sale, I knew my life could never be the same if Indie wasn't a part of it. And that terrified me.

When I stepped inside the shop that morning, I could tell she had been pacing for a while, considering she didn't even look where she walked anymore and actually had her eyes closed half the time. Though she'd spent the night in my bed while I took the couch—only after I begged her to leave her horrifying apartment behind—she'd left before I even woke up, sneaking past me without waking me. She'd probably been at the shop for hours, and she looked ready to unravel.

"Will you sit?" I asked quietly. "You're making me dizzy."

But she rolled her eyes and kept pacing. She'd obviously already cried at least once that morning and looked ready to start again unless I found a way to distract her.

"Why didn't you wake me up?" I asked, settling into a chair as I watched her. "I would have given you a ride."

"You looked way too peaceful," she replied and even managed a passable smile. "Like a puppy."

"You really need to stop comparing me to dogs," I said, though I didn't mean a word of it. If she was strong enough to insult me, she was strong enough to make it through the day. For now, that was all I needed. "Tell me about this buyer you found."

That, apparently, was the right thing to say, because it stopped her pacing and brought her into a chair next to me. "I don't know much," she admitted mournfully. "All I know is he has big plans for the space and was willing to pay the asking price, so it doesn't really matter."

"Big plans? That sounds interesting."

"It sounds awful," she replied, dropping her head onto my shoulder. "But there's nothing I can do about that."

Hesitant, I reached over and gently rubbed her knee. Over the last two days she'd gone back and forth, sometimes welcoming my touch and sometimes keeping me at a safe distance. To say she was completely confusing was an absolute understatement, and it was driving me crazy. Either she wanted to be with me or she didn't, and giving her the time to decide was a lot harder than I'd expected. I'd decided the moment she'd woken up in my lap that first night in her apartment that life without her would be miserable at best, so what was I doing wrong that she couldn't make up her mind about me?

"I know I haven't made things easy for you the last little while," she said suddenly, linking her arm through mine as she sat there.

"Have you ever?"

She jabbed her elbow into my side. "I'm serious, Matt."

Not many people called me by that nickname, and I immediately realized it sounded so much better when she said it. "You've been through a lot," I said and closed my eyes, savoring her nearness and the feel of her hands clasped around my bicep and the faint scent of coffee that always seemed to linger around her. I'd never thought much of the bittersweet smell until I realized it was hers, and then I fell in love with it.

"So have you," she argued. "You've been nothing but nice to me."

"You mean when I kept showing up here when you didn't want me to, and I made things with Zeus worse, and I very nearly got you killed because you had to come rescue my sorry butt?"

"Aside from that," she replied, and I could hear her smile. These were my favorite moments, when she was happy enough to smile and joke and be comfortable around me. There hadn't been many the last few days, and if she gave me the chance, I would spend my life trying to keep her this contented.

"But really," she said and sat up, so I opened my eyes to meet her gaze. "I may not show it very well, but I'm glad you turned up and beat the crap out of Orion that day. You almost make all of this worth it."

My heart felt like it turned to stone, a solid, painful lump in my chest. *Almost.* But not quite. Swallowing, I tried to keep my smile so she wouldn't lose hers. "So do you have a plan for after you sell the shop?" I asked. It was a very important question, and the answer would tell me a lot about the future. Our future.

Indie looked up at me with her incredible green eyes that slowly filled with tears. "I don't want to talk about that yet," she said quietly and slipped her hand in mine.

I didn't like the sound of that.

A knock at the door pulled my gaze away from her as a woman stepped inside the shop, a file of papers in her hands and a look of interest in her eyes as she glanced around. "Ms. Fierro?" she asked, barely looking at me.

Indie took a deep breath that made her look calm, but she nearly strangled my hand as she nodded. "Are you the notary?"

"I'm Samantha Gilles," she replied, coming to join us at our little table. She shook Indie's hand then glanced at me only briefly when Indie introduced me. "Shall we get started? I'm sure you're eager to get this done and settled."

Eager may have been a bit of an overstatement, but Indie nodded anyway. "Shouldn't the buyer be here?" she asked.

"Normally, yes," Samantha replied, "but he insisted I come to him earlier this morning, as he had a pressing matter he couldn't miss." Again a quick glance at me, but Indie didn't seem to notice. She was busy staring at that spot of old glue on the table and trying not to cry again.

"Let's get this over with," Indie said.

Samantha took a few minutes to explain the terms of the sale, and Indie signed each page as they went through it, though I wasn't sure how much she really listened or even looked at the pages. She was resigned to the sale, not glad of it, and all the money would just go straight to Zeus's accountant anyway. She stayed strong, though, keeping her emotions in check and barely trembling as she made each signature.

Until the last page, at least. The final signature seemed a bit too much for Indie to handle, and she sat there frozen with her pen hovering just above the paper. Would she be able to do it? The shop was her last connection to her husband, and Indie seemed convinced that signing away the shop meant she was signing away Dante.

Leaning close, I put my arm around her shoulders and held her tight. "Everything will work out," I told her softly. "Trust me."

She looked over at me, her eyes glistening with more than just sadness. Did she really trust me enough to believe me? I hoped so. Otherwise what else could I do?

Indie took another deep breath, and then she scribbled her name on the line before she lost all her bravery. And then she fell into my arms as if completely devoid of energy.

"Everything should be settled now," Samantha said, rising to her feet. *A bit too cheerful, Miss Gilles.* "I'll make sure the transfer is made, and you should receive a final receipt of sale in the next couple of days. Do you have the keys?"

Indie looked ready to crumble, but she reached into her pocket anyway and pulled out a small keychain.

"Perfect," Samantha said with a smile, and then she held the keys out to me. "Mr. Davenport, I believe these belong to you."

Indie stiffened beside me. I held my breath. Samantha smiled as she dropped the keys into my open palm.

"Matthew?" Indie whispered as she sat up. I couldn't tell if it was a good whisper or a bad one. "What did you do?"

"I made a solid business investment," I said carefully.

It was almost like she hadn't fully figured out what had just happened, and she watched Samantha tuck away all the forms and head out of the shop before she spoke again. "Are you telling me you bought my shop?" she asked.

I tried to play it off as no big deal, but I was so nervous that she would get angry with me that my shrug failed halfway. "Well, I signed the papers this morning and wrote a check, so I certainly hope so." *Please don't be mad.* I couldn't bear it if she went back to hating me.

Taking a long, slow breath, Indie got to her feet and locked her intense gaze on me. "I always knew you were an idiot," she said, "but you've managed to outdo yourself."

She was mad. *Not good.* I wasn't entirely sure how to make this better, but I knew I had to stand my ground. I folded my arms then said, "I'm pretty sure I'm smarter than you're giving me credit, Indiana."

"Don't call me that," she snapped. "You bought a failing business, Matthew."

"It was only failing because you had a bunch of morons scaring people off," I argued. "That's not a problem anymore."

"I told you I didn't want your money."

I stood so she wasn't looming over me, but that brought me close enough to her that I could see the different green hues in her eyes. That wouldn't exactly help me concentrate on my argument, but I didn't really care. "Are you backing out of the sale, Ms. Fierro?"

She turned red. "I'm not—"

"I thought you were more honest than that."

Her eyes grew wider. "That's not—"

"Now if you'll excuse me, I have a coffee shop to refurbish before its grand reopening in a few weeks. I have a lot to do."

I got about two steps before she grabbed my arm and spun me around to face her again. She couldn't seem to decide how she felt anymore, torn between smiling and scowling. Maybe I shouldn't have surprised her like this, but I knew it was the only way to make it happen without her trying to stop me. Indie was stubborn, and I desperately hoped my plan would work.

"You did this for me?" she asked quietly.

I shook my head. "I happen to really like making coffee."

Just like I knew she would, she threw her fist into my shoulder. But her tears weakened her punch, and she ended up resting her hand on my chest as she stood there. "Matthew," she begged.

I knew she wanted a serious answer, but the real answer wasn't an easy thing to say. I needed her strength, so I wrapped my fingers around hers. "I would do anything for you, Indie," I said.

"Why?"

She had to ask that question… That one word was more dangerous than she realized. Especially because I hadn't seen this coming, and there was no logical explanation, and there was no going back if I admitted it. But honestly, what did I have to lose? Only her, and if I said nothing, I would probably lose her anyway.

Here goes nothing. "Because I love you, Indie," I said. "And even if you don't feel the same way, I'm going to need you here. I'm not worried about the finance side of things for obvious reasons, but as I'm sure you're aware, I'm crap at making coffee, and—"

She grabbed my collar and leaned up on her toes, and she kissed me so suddenly that it took me a second to realize she'd done it. And then the rest of the world disappeared as I took her up in my arms and pulled her in tight, losing myself in that kiss.

Kissing her the first time had been incredible, but I'd surprised her with it then marched off to my potential death. Kissing her when she kissed me back was unfathomably better, and I didn't want to stop. It was like putting the final piece in a puzzle. Feeling a complicated lock click open after trying to pick it for several minutes. Stepping into the rain on a hot summer afternoon. Kissing Indie made me feel like the world was right again and no darkness could ever touch me.

But Indie was Indie, and she pulled away before I was ready and looked up into my face as tears slid down her cheeks.

"Where did you come from?" she whispered.

I wasn't sure I had the air to reply, so I wiped her tears with my thumbs until I could breathe again. "I just walked through the door," I said. "Don't you remember?"

Shaking her head, Indie put her arms around my neck and leaned up to kiss me again. "Such an idiot," she said against my lips.

"I love you," I replied.

Completely.

CHAPTER TWELVE

"When was the last time we had an actual barbecue?" Lanna asked, balancing way more food in her arms than we could ever eat.

I rushed to relieve her before she dropped the potato salad teetering at the top. "I'm pretty sure it was the Fourth of July three years ago when you decided Catherine should try living like a normal person for a week," I said.

"I still haven't forgiven you for that!" Catherine shouted from the picnic table ahead. But her mock glare was interrupted when Seth snuck in a kiss as he passed with a plate of hamburgers.

"Just set that on the table, Matthew," Lanna said then turned on Catherine, who was slightly pink from her encounter with her fiancé. "I only made you do it because you were mean to my favorite caterer, Catherine."

Rolling her eyes, Catherine hopped off the table to help set out the various side dishes. "To be fair," she said, "I was still killing my bad habits. Josh got over it."

"He didn't get over it," Lanna whispered to me with a smirk. "He's still afraid of her."

"Anyone who *isn't* afraid of Catherine is an idiot," I replied.

"Too true," Seth muttered without looking up from the grill, where he and Adam were prepping the meat for our Memorial Day feast.

Benny sat on Adam's shoulders, happy to watch his father at work, and Adam looked healthier than ever. Happy, even. The ladies laughed as they continued to argue back and forth. The sun shone bright through perfectly clear skies, and the park was alive with families enjoying the start of summer. I almost couldn't imagine a more perfect scene. Almost. It was only missing one thing.

"Okay, I'm starving," Catherine announced, directing the comment right at me. "When do we get to eat?"

I raised an eyebrow. "Why're you looking at me?"

"Because I know you're not going to let us lay a finger on any of this until your lady arrives."

And suddenly four pairs of eyes were on me, which sent my face burning. None of them had *really* met Indie yet, and I was more than a little nervous about the upcoming introduction. I loved my family dearly, but they could definitely be intimidating. Even without our wealth, we were a force to be reckoned with. Seth was…Seth. And Catherine not only had one of the brightest minds in the country but looked like a literal princess most of the time. (She had, thankfully, toned down her glamor for the barbecue.) Lanna was a celebrated artist and the kindest person in the world, and her husband was both incredibly famous and incredibly shy, which made him seem snobbish and overly critical. If Indie didn't run for her life, I'd call the day a success.

And there was always the chance that *they* wouldn't like *her*—how could they not?—and I would have to decide between my family and the woman I was hopelessly in love with. That was not a decision I was particularly keen to make.

To say I was nervous was about as understated as it got.

Adam handed over his tongs to Seth then lowered Benny into Lanna's arms. He had a knowing smile on his face that I didn't like at all because it meant we were about to have a heart-to-heart. I'd barely managed to talk to him since I stopped avoiding him completely, and things were still tense between us. But he put his arm around my shoulders and led me a little deeper into the park.

"I've known you for a long time, Matthew," he said, gazing out over the nearby pond where a few kids fed frozen peas to the horde of ducklings swimming around. "A really long time."

"You're making me feel old," I replied. "You make it sound like we met a hundred years ago."

"Sometimes it feels like it," he replied with a soft smile. "But that means I know you better than I think you realize. In all the years we've been friends, I've never seen you show any interest in *anyone*. And I've been worried about you."

"You and everyone else," I grumbled, stuffing my hands into my pockets.

Adam chuckled. "I didn't mean it like that. I meant… Our line of work isn't easy, and you spent so much energy keeping my family safe that you forgot about yourself and let the stress of it eat at you and wear you down."

I turned to meet his gaze, wondering where he might be going with the conversation.

"Believe it or not," he continued, "it helps to have someone share your stress sometimes. And to give you some of theirs when they need your strength. A partnership. You spend all your time saving everyone else that I think you forget to save yourself sometimes. You forget to let yourself *be* saved. If this girl makes you happy, then it doesn't matter what any of us think. You need to do what's best for you."

That sounded eerily familiar, and it wasn't until Adam gave me a crooked smile that I realized I'd given him an almost identical speech back when he was interested in Lanna. He worried what everyone else would think when he pursued someone none of them thought was worth his time. *It doesn't matter what anyone thinks as long as you're happy, Adam. As long as you both are.* And looking at what the two of them had made of their lives, it definitely seemed like good advice.

Pleased by whatever he saw on my face, Adam slowly started walking backward toward our table. "Don't let other people get in the way of your happiness, Matt," he said before joining his wife and scooping his son back into his arms.

Happiness. My family was the perfect example of that, and I watched them smile at each other and share little glances around the picnic table. And I'd never wanted what they had more than I did now. After a lifetime of thinking I didn't deserve that kind of happily ever after, I was starting to wonder.

"Has anyone ever told you your family looks perfect?" a soft voice said behind me.

My reply got lost the moment I saw her standing in the grass. Indie was always beautiful, but everything about her—her white flowy sundress and dark hair curling over her shoulder and the little freckles on her cheeks that came out more with the sun—left me absolutely breathless. "Perfect," I repeated, not completely sure what her question was.

Her blush made the not breathing thing even worse. "How do I…

Do I look okay?" she asked, glancing down at what she wore. "I wasn't sure what people like your… I don't have much to wear that isn't… I mean…" She sighed, grimacing with worry.

I crossed the small distance between us to kiss her before my motor function left me. "You look amazing," I assured her, resting my forehead against hers.

I knew my family was likely watching and wondering if I would ever bring her over, but I wanted just a moment with her on my own before I set her loose. We'd been together almost a week, most of which I'd spent at her side, but I was still terrified she would remember what she first thought of me and send me packing. I certainly hadn't made the best first impression.

"Well," Indie said and laced her fingers with mine. "I guess it's time to go into battle. And don't you dare leave me on my own. It's been way too long since I had to do something like this."

"Wouldn't dream of it," I replied.

We approached Seth first, partly because he was the most intimidating and partly because Indie had seen him before. "Indie," I said, "this is my future cousin-in-law, Seth." I was pretty sure it helped that he wore an apron that said "World's Okayest Cook" on it.

"It's a pleasure," Seth said, holding out his hand and offering her his warmest smile. Maybe a little too warm…

"Nice to, uh…" Indie's face turned a deep red, and I scowled at Seth for being so charming. "Nice to meet you," she managed to finish.

"And you remember Catherine?" I sort of growled without meaning to.

Catherine went for a hug rather than a handshake. "I'm taking credit for the two of you," she said loudly. "I was the one who suggested Matthew work for you."

"Well now it's the other way around," Indie replied. Her smile came more easily than it did with Seth, which was a good sign. "Technically he's *my* boss now."

"Never," I said and gave her hand a squeeze. "You are definitely the one giving orders. This is Adam, my brother-in-law, and my nephew, Benny."

"For your brother?" Indie asked quietly.

Could I love the woman any more? I hadn't said a thing about Ben since the cemetery a week and a half earlier, but somehow she remembered.

"It's very nice to meet you, Benny," she said to the toddler, who shyly hid in his father's shoulder. "And you," she said to Adam, shaking his hand. She seemed to be getting more and more comfortable. I hoped she was, at least.

I didn't realize it until I was about to introduce her, but I was most worried about what Lanna would think of Indie. Over the years, my little sister had started to act like an older sister, and after she showed up at my house just because she hadn't heard from me, I realized she worried about me more than I'd thought. Ever since Luke's death, when we had both lost a dear friend, we'd been extra close. If Lanna didn't like Indie, it would tear me in half.

Holding to her hand a little tighter than I probably should have, I led Indie to where Lanna sat on the edge of the picnic table bench and quietly said, "This is my baby sister, Lanna. Lanna, this is Indie."

And Lanna burst into tears, jumping up and ambushing Indie with a hug so tight that it pulled her out of my grip. What the…?

Adam simply shrugged when I looked to him for explanation, and Catherine and Seth were both way too interested to offer any insights, so I just stood there absolutely confused—and more than a little concerned—as my sister apparently tried to drown Indie in her tears.

"Sorry," Lanna said after a moment, and she pulled back with pink cheeks and a grimace. She immediately slipped into her husband's one-armed hold then said, "I didn't mean to attack you, Indie. I just… I wanted to say thank you."

Indie seemed more confused than anyone as she glanced at me. "For what?" she asked and reached out for my hand before she had to remind me I wasn't supposed to abandon her. I smiled when she relaxed as soon as our fingers met.

"For that," Lanna said and pointed to me. "For making him smile."

Heavens, woman, I smile all the time. You don't have to strangle her.

Unlike me, Indie seemed to understand Lanna's meaning, and she reached up and brushed some hair from my forehead, convincing me to never cut it short ever again. "Yeah," she said, "it's good to see some real smiles now. For a while, I wondered if he even knew how."

How to smile?

"Oh, is that why he looks different lately?" Catherine asked. *What, her too?* "I was trying to figure it out but couldn't pinpoint it."

What were they all talking about?

Indie laughed—the most beautiful sound in the world—and

touched her thumb to my lips. "You're adorable when you're confused," she said. "But you're an adorable idiot, and that's why I love you."

Everything inside me seemed to suddenly disappear, leaving me lightheaded and dizzy all at once. Did she just say…? I could have imagined it. Maybe I was dreaming those words again, like I'd done more than once over the last week.

"Sit down before you have a heart attack," Indie said, and she gently pushed me onto the bench as she sat next to me.

A heart attack was the least of my worries. If she just said what I thought she said, I was about to explode. "You like telling me what to do," I managed to say, though the words came out a bit strangled.

Grinning, she took both my hands and looked me right in the eye. "Because I love you, Matthew. Now will you stop gaping so your family can start eating?"

I had to kiss her before I could say anything, though it might have left me even more senseless than before. She had that effect a lot. "Anything for you," I replied. My life was hers, every single piece of me, and I had no intention of getting it back.

The End

Special sneak peek of Book 4 in the Simple Love Series,

In Front of Me

EXCERPT FROM *IN FRONT OF ME*

I woke with a start and immediately regretted all my life choices.

I was never going to drink again. It wasn't worth the hammer in my head and the churning in my stomach. Or maybe that was the three pieces of cheesecake. Oh lordy, I felt awful. It had been so long since I slept anywhere but on my slightly outrageously priced mattress that I'd forgotten how stiff I could get when sleeping on something like a couch, and my entire spine felt like it had melded into a single piece.

Wait. Couch. Sleep.

I sat straight up as my heart burst into double-time. What had I done? Oh man, I was way too drunk to let a man lead me into his apartment, and while I had very little memory of the night before, I could recall getting awfully snuggly with a guy I didn't even know. How stupid could I be? But a quick investigation, along with some foggy memories of Brennon pulling a blanket over me then disappearing, told me I was fine. Nothing had happened. I was stupid, but I was fine.

I might as well have been wearing a sign around my neck that said "Lissa Montgomery: Maker of Bad Decisions since Last Week." First quitting my job, and now this. I was on a roll. And I was usually so responsible…

"Brennon is a lot of things," someone said suddenly, and I gasped and turned to the stranger sitting at a kitchen table with a bowl of cereal in front of him and pain-inducing sunshine throwing him into silhouette. "But, to my never-ending disappointment, he is not a pig. So he's got that going for him."

That wasn't Brennon. While I was thinking about it, where *was* Brennon? Had he just abandoned me the moment I passed out?

As if he could read my thoughts, the Cereal Guy finished loudly chewing and said, "Like any respectable stockbroker, my dear roommate went to work on a Sunday instead of making breakfast for the pretty girl he brought home from a wedding."

Roommate. Seriously? I'd naturally assumed, given the location of his apartment and his proximity to the likes of Catherine Davenport, that Brennon wasn't exactly wanting in money. His Armani suit may have helped lead to that conclusion, so why on earth would he need a roommate? Maybe the guy was lonely.

But first things first. "He didn't bring me home," I mumbled, trying to untangle myself from the blanket over top of me. Not an easy feat with the emerald mermaid gown Catherine had dressed me in. How had I not been smart enough to change before I joined Brennon in watching…whatever it was we watched? The answer to that was clear in my pounding headache. "I live across the hall," I added.

Cereal Guy cleared his throat then dumped some more cereal into his bowl, each little piece bouncing around inside my skull as it hit the bowl. "Not that I claim to know Catherine Davenport well," he said, "but I'm pretty sure you're not her."

Well duh. Catherine was flawless, way too intelligent to accept an invitation like I had. She probably didn't even drink anymore. "She's my…" Wow, I really needed some coffee or water or a new head altogether. What was that word? "She's my new sister-in-law. I'm staying at her place until I head back to Boston."

Now where did I put my shoes?

Cereal was almost silent as he watched me dig around the blankets in search of the heels that had given me good and proper blisters, the crunch of his chewing the only sound he made. But when I kicked my toe into the coffee table and shouted a curse, he snorted half a laugh.

"Who even are you?" I demanded as I grabbed my little toe and held it tight against the pain. One shoe poked out from under the table, though, and I was pretty sure the other had to be nearby.

"Steve," he said lightly. "Bren's my best friend, even if he can be an idiot."

I had to crawl beneath the table to reach and probably looked like an idiot myself with my rear end sticking up behind me. "What's that supposed to mean?" I grunted.

"He's out there earning a living and missing all the fun here at home."

Banging my head on the table above me, I bit back another curse but only because I needed that anger to give this Steve a decent glare. "I'm glad you're entertained," I said.

"Oh, I definitely am. I don't even remember the last time I was this amused."

I wished I could see his face so I could see if it matched his cocky, manly voice, but the sun was way too bright behind him. Looking at him too closely would probably kill me with the added headache it would bring. "Do you always laugh at helpless women?"

"Just the ones who pretend they're not," he said. "Though I'm not sure I would call you helpless."

"What would you call me then?"

"Desperate."

"Excuse me?"

He laughed for real, though it sounded off. Almost wrong. Like he'd forgotten how to do it properly. "Don't get me wrong," he said. "I'm sure you're very smart and capable. But you could do so much better than Brennon Ashworth." If he wasn't struggling to hold back his laughter, I'd almost think he was serious. And for some reason that made me smile. Only a true best friend would say something like that, and it was clear he thought very highly of Brennon.

"Well thanks for the warning," I said, finally locating my other shoe and moving to the door, where my keys hung on a handy little hook. *Thanks, Brennon.* "I'll be sure to tell him you said so." I had no intention of seeing Brennon again, though, since my flight was later that day. He would just have to be a pleasant and somewhat alarming memory. Proof that I wasn't a lost cause but should probably work on my self-control before I got myself into trouble.

"Happy to oblige," Steve replied, and when I glanced back before stepping out into the hallway, I caught a glimpse of a smile in the sunlight.

So maybe Brennon wasn't what I thought he was. He hadn't taken advantage of me last night, and his best friend obviously thought well of him. And while he wasn't exactly original with his pickup lines and advances, at least he was honest. And sympathetic. It was too bad I wasn't staying longer, or I might actually consider seeing if maybe he—

I froze at Catherine's door, staring at the note that had been taped at almost exactly my eye level:

While I enjoyed last night, I'd love the chance to get to know you a little when you're sober. Meet me for brunch? - Bren

Whoa. Never mind the dude left me a handwritten note—and had impeccably neat handwriting—but I couldn't remember the last time a man had actually *wanted* to meet sober me after meeting the much less uptight drunk me. Was Brennon Ashworth even real?

My head hurt, my back ached, and I had a flight in a few hours, but as I stood there looking at the time and place he suggested and thinking about how much I wanted to see his ridiculously handsome smile again, I was quickly running out of reasons why I shouldn't spend my last few hours in California with him. What would I do otherwise? Flip through TV channels and sip a sports drink until my cab arrived to bring me back to my big fat load of nothing in Boston.

Coffee and quiche with an attractive guy sounded a whole lot better.

ABOUT THE AUTHOR

Dana LeCheminant has been telling stories since she was old enough to know what stories were. After spending most of her childhood reading everything she could get her hands on, she eventually realized she could write her own books too, and since then she always has plots brewing and characters clamoring to be next to have their stories told. A lover of all things outdoors, she finds inspiration while hiking the remote Utah backcountry and cruising down rivers. Until her endless imagination runs dry, she will always have another story to tell.

www.ingramcontent.com/pod-product-compliance
Lightning Source LLC
Chambersburg PA
CBHW032032180726
48284CB00008B/2560